A “Creole' Chef” with a touch of Cajun

ORLEANS CATERING

Show this coupon at Orleans Catering and receive **$2.00 off** one of their popular Southern ‘carry-out' dishes.

See bottom page 11, then say hello to chef Harold in person

6703 Suitland Rd, Suitland, MD 20746 * Phone 301)967-3618

OUT
IN THE
OPEN

by

Roy E. Howard

AuthorHouse™
1663 Liberty Drive, Suite 200
Bloomington, IN 47403
www.authorhouse.com
Phone: 1-800-839-8640

First published by AuthorHouse 11/20/2007

ISBN: 978-1-4343-4917-0 (sc)

Library of Congress Control Number: 2007908444

Printed in the United States of America
Bloomington, Indiana

This book is printed on acid-free paper.

This project is *dedicated to*

my mother, Ruth Frazier Howard and my uncle George Beamon, both of whom has passed on. I thank them both for having the most profound impact on my life, and the life changing wisdom that they took the time to share with me.

Acknowledgment

I'd like to thank God for the strength it took to endure the ups and downs involved in the process, as well as for the ability to see this project through to the end.

Much love goes out to my wife, Anna Smith Howard, for holding down the fort while I pursued a dream, and for believing in my ability to fulfill it. I love you, and know that it wasn't easy.

To my son, Renwick E. Howard, for providing nothing but the best reference materials to be found, and for consulting me on the latest street jargon when I was at a loss for words. I love you, brah.

To my son, Rogers B. Howard, for his support, and understanding that I had to do this. I love you.

To my brothers, Earl "Silky" Frazier and Larry "Computer hands" Howard, for listening to my chatter and helping me with the dream. I love you both.

Finally, I'd like to spread plenty of love all around for my sister Elizabeth 'Calle' Howard in Texas, Ann Howard in California, my brother Ray Howard in California, and Irvin "Crick" Mathews of New Orleans, La. And as sure as my sisters, Ollie H. Wardy and Laura H. Cooper are looking down on us all, we love you both always.

OUT
IN THE
OPEN

1

"Girl, you've been like a horny little goat since the tenth grade," Sara said, "and just because I don't talk about boys all day doesn't mean that something's wrong with my sexuality," she concluded with strong convictions.

"I know, girl, I'm just saying," Tabora replied. "Just because I have a hardier sex drive then you doesn't mean that there's something's wrong with me either."

The two friends stared at each other in a brief moment of silence that was broken when Tabora's eyes looked away and followed the butt of a young man who'd just passed their table.

"I don't know girl, I think you're a freak." Sara finally said jokingly, and the two of them laughed.

"Seriously, though," said Tabora. "You mean you really don't have those kinda feelings inside of you that I just described?"

"I'm serious, if I did I would say so." Sara admitted.

Tabora suddenly stared quietly at Sara, then smiled when she had thoughts about all the conversations she and Sara has had while growing up together.

Today, however, in suburban Maryland, they sat in the comfort of the Cental Avenue McDonald's, where they've always met to laugh and enjoy lunch together. When Tabora thought about it, she realized that nothing much had changed between the two of them except for the fact they'd grown older; hell, she was still hot and horny, and Sara, well, when Tabora really thought about it, Sara had always seemed indifferent where sex and boys were concerned; to Tabora, her friend Sara was just a nun-like individual who seemed to have a lackluster sex drive.

On the other hand, Tabora had learned earlier in life that she was full speed ahead sexually, and endured uncontrolled yearnings for love more often than not. And she had no reason to believe that hers was anything but normal, which is until she began hearing girls her own age when they describe their, mild by comparison, sexual urges; it floored Tabora to discover that no one in their small group of friends ever described having any of the pressing sexual desires that had manifested deep within her.

Though deeply concerned about her overwhelming sexual woes, Tabora found comfort in her closely regarded friendship with Sara; with Sara she was able to reveal many of her true inner feelings about sex, but in a joking manner. The two girls had been friends since grade school, and as of today there were only two months left before they would graduate high school. Along the way the two friends had been through a lot of growing pains, and shared them all with each other, well almost all. For years now Tabora felt bad about not telling anyone of the inner sensations that drove her to the naughty behavior that she still carried on to this day.

It started in the eight-grade when Tabora began having strong sexual desires. Feelings so severe that it frightened her, and those heated desires seemed to regulate her body by sowing notions deep within, and left her longing for sex. But she never told anyone, not even Sara.

It wasn't until they reached senior high school that Tabora began delving deeper into Sara's head about Sara's own sexuality; Tabora found that compared to Sara's sex drive, hers was indeed likened to that of a horny goat; she began to think of Sara as a really bad comparison, and would tease Sara about it all the time; it seemed Sara had a fetish for licking her lips and closely admiring other girls; now when Tabora thinks about it, she feels that she spent so much time protecting the seriousness surrounding her own situation, that it never occurred to her back then that Sara may have been harboring secrets of her own. To this day she's still not sure of what to make of her friend Sara's preferences, and knowing wouldn't change their friendship in one way or the other. Her own situation had become much too serious over the years to have any worries about anyone else.

In spite of a healthy appetite for sex, to put it mildly, Tabora never viewed herself as some sort of freak or whore, though she and Sara would laugh and joke about it all the time. She began to realize, however, that her sexual needs could possibly make it impossible to carry on what was viewed by many in society to be a normal sex life. And the terms, freak, and whore, which she and Sara normally joked about, began to frighten her; if she was with a boy each time her body screamed for sex, she felt that she would certainly be labeled as some sort of school yard slut. Consequently, she'd managed to satisfy her feelings, her needs. And for all those past years of living with the starving sex monster inside of her, she felt good about the method she used to compensate for remaining a virgin.

Still, as bad as she wanted the touch of a real man's body against hers when in her dark room alone at night, she was always afraid that it would lead to the exposure of her desperate need for sex, and herself being misconstrued as some common whore. She thought more of herself than that, and to protect herself she masturbated regularly growing up, which also served as an alternative to satisfying the powerful desire to have sex.

When out in public, the mere sighting of someone as vaguely as an unknown passer by could trigger lust, and Tabora would unconsciously shake her legs in and out nervously. Through years of the episodes, she'd finally made the connection between the lustful sightings and the shaking of her legs, but that also became something she didn't care to discuss with anyone, and she blocked it out.

Tabora was older now and felt that masturbation had always been satisfying to her while growing up, but now that she'd come of age it had finally run its course; she now longed for the loin of a man deep inside of her, a man's touch, to brush her hardened nipples.

These days she still keeps her secrets close to her heart, as far as sharing them with Sara, but she finds herself flirting more openly with men, and today at the McDonald's restaurant was just another day in the life of young Tabora.

She sipped soda from her cup through the straw in the center of the lid, then leaned closer to Sara, who sat directly across the table.

Sara instinctively knew that Tabora was about to speak, and abruptly stopped her.

"Before you say anything, girl, let me say this: please stop that," Sara's said, then looked down beneath the table.

"Stop what?"

"Stop shaking your legs, girl," Sara replied. "Why is it you do that again?"

"I Told you I didn't know, it's just habit. Seriously though, I want to tell you something." Tabora insisted.

"No. Serious to you, Tabora, at least stop shaking the damn table," Sara said.

"Okay. Now listen, do you ever think about just screwing some poor fool to death?" Tabora asked in no uncertain terms.

"Ooh, hh, Tabora," Sara said, she shook her head slowly from side to side.

"What?"

"That mouth of yours," Sara said, then smiled humbly. Her eyes swept the nearby tables. Customers seated nearby showed no sign of over hearing Tabora's intrusive question, then Sara added. "I think about boys if that's what you mean . . . but it's never to that extent." Sara concluded, then smiled. She suddenly stopped smiling when she noticed Tabora's far away stare glaring beyond her right shoulder.

. . . Just that fast Tabora was distracted. She had not heard a word of the lie that Sara told of having thoughts of boys. Instead, her mind and eyes were focused lustfully on the young man who had entered McDonald's and stood on line to be waited on.

"Don't look now," Tabora said, "but the boy in the blue shirt over there, tell me you wouldn't want to do the nasty with him. . . ." Tabora reached over and tugged Sara excitedly.

"There, look at him now, girl."

"Damn, 'ho, what are you eating over there, a horny burger?" shouted Sara. "Besides, that's Chad. He thinks he's cute if you ask me. I hear he's got his own place, though, and throws wild parties there . . . I think he sells drugs too" –

"You mean you know him?" Tabora asked, wide eyed. Nothing Sara had said about Chad affected Tabora's desire to get to know him better. She watched him while licking the tip of her index finger then place her finger between her lips before slowly licking it again.

The young man appeared to notice the sexual overtones of Tabora's sexually explicit display; she sucked and licked her finger tellingly, while her inviting eyes intertwined with his from afar.

"No, I don't exactly know him," confessed Sara. "And . . . wait, what are you doing?" Sara asked, when Tabora raised her right hand and beckoned the young man over to the table.

"Don't call him over here. What is wrong with you?" Sara placed her lowered forehead in the cup of her right hand. She did not believe Tabora's hot, desperate ass could ever be so common.

Still, the stranger loomed over the table, his crotch was eye level to Tabora and her telling eyes shone with lust; Sara's cold, eerie stare caught Tabora's gleaming eyes locked on the print of the young man's bulging crotch.

"Hello, ladies," the stranger said.

His eyes trailed Tabora's right hand down to her exposed right thigh when she brazenly crossed her legs beneath the small table; Tabora was turned on by the stranger's aggressive eyes, and wanted him to see more of her. She tightened her crossed right leg causing the cheek of her butt to be exposed to him, then she lied.

"Hi, we remember you from school, Chad," said Tabora.

Chad smiled and glanced toward Sara, then back to Tabora, "Yeah, from school, huh? And you are?"

"Oh," Tabora said, forgetting her manners. Her perfectly aligned white teeth and large hazel eyes were set to charm Chad further. "I'm Tabora and this is my friend, Sara."

"That's too pretty a name, Sara, but why are you sitting there looking so down. You can show a brother a smile, or something," said Chad before he smoothed his dread-locked hair with his right hand, then pushed his glasses up to the bridge of his nose with his right index finger.

"Chad, nothing personal dear, but I'm doing just fine sitting here minding mine," Sara snapped her response, then added, "You perhaps might wanna pay more attention to the big smile on Tabora's face, she's the one who called you over here."

"I feel you, babe. My bad," Chad said, then, as suggested, he turned his full attention back to Tabora, "So Tabora, what' you up to, girl?" he asked. "Check-it-out, I've got some pressing business right now, but I would certainly like to have your number. Who knows, maybe we can hookup and do something later," he said and smiled again, in Sara's direction.

Sara, nonetheless, stared under eyed at Tabora like a hungry lioness at prey.

Tabora could feel the heat, but chose to ignored Sara's vicious, laser charged stare and defiantly indulged Chad.

"Okay," Tabora said, then cleared her throat, "but why don't you let me have your number," she countered.

She wrote Chad's number on a napkin and dropped it into her purse. After a moment of small talk, they ended their encounter. She stared hard at his butt as he departed, leaving a pleasant trail of Domain cologne dancing in her nostrils. "Um, mm, that boy smells good," she muttered.

"I don't know, girl, that brother is fine," Tabora said as she fell helplessly against the back of her chair, her head drifted backward and to the right. She was as satisfied as a woman after good sex, and massaged her left shoulder softly with her right hand, then unconsciously grabbed a tight fist full of her blouse sleeve. She exhaled hard while slithering from side to side in her seat. Tabora uncrossed her legs and began shaking them again, this time with her right arm pressed against her crotch.

"Ooh, girl, seriously, he doesn't turn you on?" Tabora asked.

"No." Sara said. "And don't you ever again, as long as you're black, involve me in any of your, 'little girl meets boy pranks'. Do you hear me, girl?"

Tabora sensed Sara's anger and couldn't understand why. The two of them could usually joke their way through any situation. Lately, though, whenever there was a man involved, Sara seemed to get heated, down right upset. Men, it seemed had begun to drive a wedge between them. Confused. Tabora's smile slowly subsided. She didn't see any harm in what she'd done, and couldn't believe Sara's angry reaction. Those were the type reactions from Sara that made Tabora feel that perhaps she was some sort of freak when it came to men. Why else would Sara be so upset, she thought?

Since the eight-grade Tabora wanted to discuss her situation with her parents, but refused to because everything she'd ever discussed with them previously sent them into shock, it seemed, and left them all bent out of shape: "you'd better keep your mind on your books, little girl, and forget about those damn boys," her parents would say. Or, "There's nothing wrong with you child, little girls go through that," her mother would say privately, before ending with her most famous line of all. "You better not bring any babies into this house, I know that much," her mother would say.

Her parents, she felt, were always too busy to address her problems. Now her best friend seemed offended and Tabora didn't know how to explain to Sara what it's been like living with the feelings she had been keeping to herself for all those years. She grimaced and silently faced Sara.

"I was just playing, and I didn't mean to upset you, okay?" Tabora said, forcing a superficial smile, she stood and added, "I almost forgot too, I have to meet my dad at the house. I'll see you later, okay."

Tabora left the table immediately, before the wells of her eyes over flowed with tears.

Sara scowled at first, then she seemed to realize the seriousness of Tabora's sudden departure. "Tabora? Girl, what is it?" Sara yelled out to her while turned around in her seat.

Tabora turned and waved to Sara. She felt she had been taking a beating from Sara and other close friends, each time she mentioned sex, and now she needed her space. She thought a little time to herself would do her good, allow her to give thought to possible resolutions to her body's ever present needs.

* * *

Two weeks later, and Tabora had spoken with Sara only once on the phone, though they spoke civilly whenever they met in school. Soon after came their graduation, and they reconciled their differences, but their post graduation priorities kept them apart more than ever before. Sara zipped around from place to place in preparation for the four years of college that stood before her, which didn't leave much time for socializing. Tabora, on the other hand, sought employment in the District's competitive work place during the day. There were lots of promising leads, but she remained a statistic of the unemployed.

Though their time together was limited, Tabora still used Sara's name on occasions when she wanted to get out of the house during the early evening; that is, without being scrutinized by her mother's motherly concerns; that evening she had already set the stage for her departure.

She left her home in Camp Springs, after telling her mother she would head to the mall after meeting up with Sara; she could have kicked herself for lying to her mother again. This would be her third such venture, twice before she went out walking alone and both those trips seemed promising; the burning desires inside of her had finally taken its toll, but each of the prior times her nerves failed her. She now longed to take real action toward some form of physical satisfaction. Tabora's first two times out made her feel like a young star. She received all the attention from men passing along the street where she pretended to be out for a walk.

Fear of the unknown had kept her from indulging in any physical contact on those first two trips out, but this time she wanted more than fan fare from a man.

All alone under the baby blue and grey skies of dusk, Tabora walked along Suitland Road. It was a long thorough fare that connected two major highways at either end, and due to the various shops and restaurant along the strip, lots of people cruised through in their vehicles in search of one thing or another. This evening, however, young Tabora was doing some searching all her own.

So young and inexperienced, Tabora had no way of knowing that her amateurish mannerism exposed her age; her eyes peered toward every passing vehicle to see who might look her way, while smiling. Her body language exposed her desires; she strutted that slender butt confidently along the concrete 'cat walk' and blushed openly as she attracted attention of men young and old.

Car horns sounded from young and older men alike, while others shouted desires from passing vehicles. Still, some men pulled to the curb right away, others made the block, it seemed, and returned to give her their best shot.

"Hey, baby, you need a ride?" the stranger said as he swiftly pulled to the curb beside Tabora.

"No, thank you, I'm fine," she replied.

"I can see that, sweetheart . . . Check this out, though, you trying to get into something or you just slinging that ass for the hell of it?"

She blushed in a way that told every man who passed that she was young yet ready to be taken.

One stranger after the other made attempts to reign in the young inexperience beauty for themselves, and she resisted, but cold heartedly. Men, it seemed, became angry. Tabora quickly learned of the power she possessed; she was a man's magnet. If she played herself correctly, it stands to reason she could've picked or chose any man she desired – but who was she fooling? Beside her desire to finally satisfy the raging monster inside of her, she had no knowledge of what to expect from a man.

She had no idea what she was doing on the fast track. She thought about it briefly and determined she was going to experience some form of pleasure before the night was over, regardless of her fears. Nervous, because the longer she walked and didn't allow herself to be picked up, the conversations seemed to get hostel. She quickly lied, in hopes of buying herself some time.

"I'm just going up the street to a friend's house, thank you," she said.

"Yeah, right, I've seen you out here before, teasing. You better get your young, fine ass home to your daddy, 'ho, before your ass is sorry you didn't," the stranger advised her as he peeled away from the curb. He seemed to purposely shower her with road pebbles from his tires.

The obscene conversations from one motorist, it turned out, rattled Tabora. She needed some place to go, to think for a moment. Still, she was not prepared to go home. Moreover, in her careless haste to find a safe haven, she didn't notice the white van as it passed her by then turned around.

She found herself standing outside of 'Orleans Catering', a popular restaurant serving southernly styled Ribs, Chicken, and Fish dinners, as only Chef Harold could prepare. Hence, the many patrons outside in front of the restaurant, seated in their automobiles and at the outdoor seating areas where they enjoyed their meals while piping hot.

She pretended to use the outdoor telephone when she spotted the white van. It had pulled to the curb in front of the auto body shop next door to Orleans Catering.

The driver sat momentarily, Tabora could see that the brown skinned man inside of the van openly watched her. Nervous. She wondered if this was it, her first encounter with a man, her first opportunity to satisfy her body's yearning desires. She did not know how encounters of a sexual nature between men and women were initiated, but she felt the van seemed a nice cozy place to be with a man.

From where she stood, the man inside the van seemed just what her heart desired; he looked to be fine, and had long stringy black hair. As she stood staring toward him, she could only dream of the many ways he could satisfy her body's yarning. However, when she heard the sound of the engine, after the man started the van, she panicked. *Why doesn't he call me over?* She wondered. She knew he wanted her. She could feel it; by then she could feel him. Her heart pounded recklessly. Filled with confusion, she watched as the van began to slowly move away. She told herself that there was no more time to think about it . . . this was her time, and she wanted to spend it with him.

She let the receiver fall from her right hand, then beckoned with her left hand for the van to stop. She ran to the van and the stranger driving it as if drawn to him telepathically, and opened the door with no questions asked. She jumped into the van before it slowly drove away.

After their initial salutations they swopped small talk, that is until Tabora felt compelled to push the conversation along in her attempts to appear older and knowledgeable.

"So, Emanuel, are you a Puerto Rican," she asked as she glanced over her left shoulder at the vastly empty space in the rear of the van. When her head turned back, her eyes swept down to his bulging crotch and she squeezed her legs tightly together at the sight.

"Yah . . . se, you like Puerto Rican men, no?" he asked.

Tabora noticed his wide, roaming eyes as they stared between her long swaying legs beneath every street light they passed; her short jean skirt provided little cover for the sight of her panties left by the motion of her fast-moving legs. They fanned in and out, over and over again. Emanuel must have read her like a book, when he reached over aggressively with his right hand. He began to slowly massage her firm, titillating breast.

Instinctively she pushed his hand away, yet in a playful way that left him knowing that she wanted his warm touch all over her body.

"Ooh, you like breast, huh?" Tabora whispered while unbuttoning her blouse. She smiled and reached her right hand behind her back to release the snap of her bra. She settled into her seat, her legs swung open and closed, slow and smooth at first. Emanuel cautiously reached his right-hand back over and fondled her breast, and this time he met no resistance – it instantly turned her on. She tried all she knew how to talk through the tender brushes of his hand against her hard nipple, but failed clumsily when the sensation rippled deep down inside of her.

"I've heard lots of good things about how you Puerto Ricans can make sweet love to a woman," she lied, then moaned openly. "Oh, hh, wee, ee, shit." The touch of his hand was everything she'd dreamed it would, when alone in her dark room.

She leaned back in her seat and began rubbing the insides of her thighs. On the ball of both her feet, she raised her knees as high as they could go. They slowly bumped together against her own groping hand between her legs. She closed her eyes and worked the two fingers of her right hand gently between her legs and began masturbating; her private habit had unwittingly followed her into the open, and she quickly closed her eyes and enjoyed herself immensely. Just as she would in her dark bedroom.

Her torso pumped up and down in short, quick strokes against her fingers. Her knees seemingly swung open and close to a rhythm, in time with her short, quick strokes. She had never felt anyone else's hand on her hard nipples before, or anywhere else on her body, but it was all that she had imagined it to be. Her mind, body and soul were aloft from the sensation. Tabora squeezed her legs tightly together and moaned aloud once more. "Oh, hh, damn, Emanuel," she cried.

Hearing his name appeared to make Emanuel grasp her breast hard, and he seemed to go into a frenzy. His eyes swept the curb side frantically, seeking some place to pull the van over to.

Tabora grinded faster, and faster, and peeked over at the print of his hard rod under the cover of darkness while stroking herself. Then she screamed. She exhaled with the look of satisfaction on her shiny face, she slowly rounded her lips, wetting them with her tongue, then smiled.

Emanuel must have gotten excited. She noticed him abruptly pull the van into a vacant lot a distance pass where he'd picked her up. She nervously gathered herself.

"Why are you stopping here?" She asked, in a soft tone. She did not want to appear eager to fuck, but she was ready.

Emanuel's touch had already caused her insides to sizzle; she had already envisioned him on top of her, and even inside of her when she masturbated. Her young mind had told her to wait for his strong aggressive arms to take her to the back and lay her down, and she did. It took every muscle in her body to keep her in her seat; she wanted him now, yet she wanted badly to show restraint as she felt an older, experience woman would.

Suddenly something went terribly wrong, though. She screamed in pain; Emanuel had grabbed and squeezed her breast in a sudden violent rage. He continued to get rough as he stepped to the rear of the van and attempted to pull her to the back by force. His scowl and the cold, and eerie look in his eyes revealed his intentions; she told herself that he was going to rape her, and perhaps kill her if she didn't make a move to escape now. She couldn't understand what it was she'd done to him to make him turn on her with such violence.

"You like Puerto Ricans, is that right, whore you?" Emanuel said, with a voice like ice. He continued his assault.

"Come, this you Mexican lover is here."

"Stop, what are you doing?" she yelled. She held on tightly to the rear of her seat. Finally she let out a loud scream.

"Let me go, you motha fucka." Tabora managed to get her right hand free. To her own surprise, she punched Emanuel hard to the face. She paused momentarily and watched as Emanuel's own weight along with the force of her punch sent him stumbling backwards toward the rear door. She scrambled nervously to let herself out of the van then ran as fast as she could to escape his terror. The van started up moments later, Tabora panicked and stumbled clumsily but was up and running immediately. When she looked back, however, the van hopped abruptly then peeled away in the other direction.

Still frightened of what could've happened to her, she moved quickly and wondered what she should do next. It'll soon be dark and she couldn't call her parents. She walked back toward 'Orleans Catering'. Her pace quickened as she walked toward the oncoming traffic. Darkness quickly draped the area, most of the 'mom and pops' shops along the street were closed in the area where she walked. The invitations, however, were still coming in from passers-by.

"Damn, girl, how old are you," one man asked from the other side of the street, driving slowly. "Are you alright? You need a ride somewhere?"

"No," Tabora shouted, "I'm okay, thank you."

She looked rough; her long length hair fluffed upward in the back of her head and danced wildly about the front. Her black bra straps swung from the tight fist of her left hand while she struggled to button her blouse. Fear masked her face, and the fast pace she maintained reflected the concern she felt for her safety. She looked in both directions of Suitland Road before rushing across to the other side; her right arm was firmly against her breast. She thought about packing it in and going home, but that was not a real option. Tabora was determined that this was going to be her night out. She wiped the tears that lingered in the wells of her eyes and had just begun to calm herself when she screamed in panic.

A speeding vehicle pulled to the curb next to her. It slid along several feet before it came to a screeching halt along side of her. The man inside bore down on his horn, then shouted, "Whore. Ness time I get you." The voice shouted.

Tabora was frantic. She jumped against the metal fence along the side walk at the sound of the brakes and horn. She released a loud scream when she saw that it was Emanuel.

"Leave me alone," she yelled. She looked both ways. No cars were coming and there was no one insight to help her. She screamed to the top of her voice a second time.

The white van peeled its tires again, this time in departing. Tabora ran back across the street and headed quickly back toward Orleans Catering; she saw people moving about down there.

After her hasty retreat, Tabora remembered Chad and the phone number that he gave to her; if she could get Chad to come and get her, she would be rid of Emanuel. She rushed to the nearest phone. Unashamed of her actions, yet Tabora knew that she could never let anyone close to her ever know of her sexual escapades. This shit has to remain my little secret, she finally thought.

2

"I'm so glad you could meet me," she said as they drove away, "I couldn't wait to see you so I thought I'd give you a call, that's okay huh?" Tabora lied. She had dressed herself, made herself up and was back to her young beautiful self again. It didn't matter about Emanuel anymore. She was happy in the company of Chad.

"Yeah, it's cool you called me, babe," Chad replied. His shiny eyes assessed what he could see of her desirable young figure seated to his right. "You wanna roll to the crib with me and hangout a while?" He finally asked.

Just the sound of his voice was comforting to her, and she smiled immediately.

"Sure, that sounds good to me." She settled into her seat, released a sigh of relief –

"You a'ight over there, woman?" Chad asked.

She figured he must have heard her sigh of relief, as she sat with her long legs brushed against the front of the seat. Her knees seemed high in the air; her short skirt revealed her panties each time her knees opened and closed nervously. She watched with pleasure as Chad openly stared between her legs at every opportunity. She placed her right arm between her legs, pressed against her crotch. Under the shadow of darkness, her warm inner thighs squeezed against her arm as tight as a vice; she wanted Chad.

"Yes, I'm all right now," Tabora said softly. She leaned to her left and placed her left hand slowly inside of Chad's right thigh. She observed his receptiveness to her every passionate glide across his hard print; she also, for the first time, noticed the effect grasping a hand full of a man's hard dick had on her, even though it was still concealed. She wanted to resort to masturbation, the only thing she'd ever known – but Chad interjected. His hope was that she knew what her actions meant, because she'd succeeded in arousing him, and now she had to complete what she'd started.

"Don't tease a man, babe," Chad said, then added in a whisper, "Go-on down and handle your business."

Stunned. Tabora stared quizzically at first, then licked her lips wet. In as much as she didn't want to appear to be an inexperience idiot, she wasn't quite sure of what Chad meant. So she asked.

"You mean you want me to suck your dick?"

Chad smiled, took his eyes off the road, momentarily, and looked her in the eye. "Yeah, babe, I'd love to feel your mouth on me." Chad said; he guided her head carefully down to his crotch with his right hand around the back of her neck, and his eyes on the road in front of him.

This was an unexpected request, and like making love, she had no experience with performing either of them. The only thing she'd ever done sexually with her mouth, besides kissing, happened when she'd lick her own hard nipples in the darkness of her bed room while masturbating. But how hard could it be, she thought.

Suddenly her thoughts shifted, and she began to wonder if she was still in control of the situation. In her young mind as long as she felt in control of the situation, then it was her decision to do whatever it was she'd done. Why was he force feeding her with his dick? It's not that she didn't want to wrap her mouth around it, instead, she just wasn't sure if sucking his dick was something she should have known to do, without him telling her? To satisfy her own desires to have him in her mouth, and also to regain control of the situation, Tabora resisted momentarily. She removed his hand from her neck, threw her head to the left to remove the fallen hair from her head away from her left eye. She smiled confidently then slid her body closer to him. She opened his shirt and trousers, exposing the huge print of his rigid rock.

"Oh hh, shit," she muttered below her breath, when the street lights reflected off of his bulging underwear.

Like a deer in head lights, she stared for a moment with her mouth opened, then quickly caught herself; she hoped that Chad didn't notice her immature reaction to seeing the bulky print of a man's rod close up for the first time in her life, and she quickly continued her run of passion. Her soft lips tenderly brushed his neck and his chest, then her tongue manipulated his hard right nipple. Chad quickly reached down and unleashed his rod in anticipation of what was to come. She worked her way down until, to her surprise, she felt the hard muscle pressed firmly against her cheek. She passionately rubbed her cheek against it with her eyes closed then turned and placed it sideways between her lips. She slowly slid her warm mouth upward until she reached the top, and like a child with a lolly pop, she locked her warm mouth firmly around the head of his penis.

Her inexperience leaped out immediately after she literally sucked it like a lolly pop, and Chad protested.

"C' mon, girl, don't just suck it," he said, "work that shit, now, damn."

Tabora's head sprung upward, and she roared. "I know how to do it, shit." She lied and went back down, desperately wanting to give the impression that she knew what she was doing.

This time, with it firmly in her mouth, her head bobbed up and down slowly. Her ears twitched. She thought she heard him moan, and she turned it on more – It did her all the good in the world to hear Chad moaning and cussing to her every wet, warm stroke. She knew enough now to keep doing what she was doing, but all the excitement caused her own body began to hunger for love.

She swung her right hand over toward her thighs only to feel Chad's hand as it slid between her opened legs. Her body shivered at his first touch; she had never felt any one's touch but her own down there. His fingers were much larger than hers, and the difference made her feel good. She stroked his fingers quickly, and with each tender movement of his finger inside of her, she reciprocated with her mouth. Soon she moaned, then raised her head momentarily when his finger circled softly inside of her before penetrating deeper.

"Oh hh fuck," she blurted out loud, closed her eyes with her head leaned back against his right shoulder. She went into a vicious rage, her pelvis pumped hard against his fingers. But in all of her joy, she'd forgotten about Chad's cold, wet stick she'd left dangling in the darkness.

"C'mon girl, damn," Chad reminded her. "Get on back down there, now!"

"Uh, hh, okay," she moaned, her words were badly slurred. She hurried back down in a passionate rage as she reached her climax. She stopped, with him still in her mouth, to enjoy the moment, intermittently. "Uh, shit," she cried with her mouth full, then came up for air.

But each time she went back down on him it was with more vigor than before. Soon after she'd finally tasted his juices.

Having just crossed a pivotal point in her young life, and were certain that she'd handled her business to Chad's satisfaction, Tabora held on tightly to his right arm, with her head pressed against his shoulder, as they crossed the parking lot and headed to his second floor apartment.

To her surprise, however, there were two of Chad's friends inside listening to music and playing video games in his living room. They smoked pot and drunk liquor while playing the game. She was the least bit worried, though. She was with her man and those were his friends.

"Fellas, meet Tabora," said Chad, nonchalantly, he then added, "Tabora, meet the fellas."

"Hi precious, I'm Baby Chris," the younger one said, "you wanna ride this blunt?" he asked. The joint was clutched between the tips of his thumb and index fingers of his out stretched right hand. She smiled gingerly as she stared down at the joint, then replied, "No thanks . . . Baby Chris, I don't smoke, but you go on and enjoy your self."

By then Danny stood directly in front of her. He stared at her from her cleavage to those long legs that ran down from her short skirt. Danny rubbed his bearded chin with his right hand. Finally their eyes met and he extended his right hand to shake hers, "Babe oh babe, I'm Danny, okay Boo-boo, and if there's anything you think you might need just holla-back, girl, cause I'm here for you,"

She laughed while retrieving her right hand from Danny's clutches, then said. "Thanks, Danny, I'll keep that in mind –

"Oh, by the way, do you wanna shot of Scotch? You know, to release the inner soul," Danny said sarcastically. He held the half empty bottle up for her to see.

"No thanks fellas, I'll just walk to the back by Chad's . . . holler," she said jokingly as she proceeded to the back in search of Chad. In the process, though, a devious smile adorned her face when she turned and looked back at the fellas, who stood wide eyed, likened to two statues.

Their glassy eyes fixated on the dye-tie jean skirt that tightly supported her firm curved ass.

She opened the last door on the left and peeked into a solid wall of darkness.

"Come on in, girl, shit," Chad yelled, "and closed the door." The fragrance of the room danced about her sense of smell, a mood setting fragrance, indeed, like a 'scent shop', she thought, with countless scented oils, Jasmine, Violet and others. Instantly transcended. Her insatiable sexual urges began to guide her emotions. She stood with both her arms extended out in front of her, like feelers, then she exhaled hard and said in a low seductive whisper, "I can't see you but I'm feeling you all inside of me."

"I know, babe," Chad replied in a voice that came from her right, eight feet away, "now part with those clothes, and walk toward my voice."

Her heart pounded nervously, at first. Still, she quickly headed in the direction of his voice. There was the sense of mysticism in the air. The darkness reminded her of the countless nights she had laid in her own dark bedroom naked, massaging herself between her legs, feeling herself. There was always complete darkness in her bedroom, no faces, no one to answer to. After all, she could only imagine the flesh, friction, and mad sex involved in love making when she masturbated.

She had never had a lover, a real man atop her flesh, within her flesh. Emanuel had tarnished her perception of what she thought her first man would be. Chad, she thought, was every bit of the man she felt she would ever need during her wildest fantasies.

As a result, her eyes were closed. She lay atop the freshly scented sheet, moaning. Feelings inside of her caused her body to twist in every direction with Chad's every tender touch, kiss, and nibble of her hard nipples. When she felt herself almost coming, she panicked.

"*Ooh, shit,*" she muttered, her body shuddered, "put it in, *please,*" she begged Chad not to tease her. She anxiously awaited the moment when his rock solid rod would pierce the walls of her hot wet cavity down below.

Yet his warm wet lips kept finding places on her body that released feelings she never knew existed. Her head slowly rolled from side to side while her body snaked up and down, almost out of control, finally she screamed, "Fuck me, shit."

"Shut the fuck up, bitch, I got this," Chad said, "Now, do you want it?"

"Yes, now stop playing," she said, "Ooh, shit, wait, wait," she cried out before she stopped to reposition her body, "Okay," she whispered.

Chad appeared to have had to struggle to barely penetrate her and voiced his discontent.

"Damn girl, this shit is tight," he said, then he pierced further. She moaned, lifted her butt and slowly swerved her hips from side to side. She wanted him inside of her, but good.

"Oh, shit, wait," Chad shouted, before he suddenly plunged deep inside of her with full force. She screamed out loud, "ugh, damn, Chad," a painful cry, at first, but then she realized she indeed wanted every inch of him right where he was. She settled in and began to slowly reciprocate.

She cried joyously and held him tighter in her arms. Her pace quickened automatically with his, and when she felt him releasing inside of her and penetrating ever deeper, she stopped and let out a long sigh. Still, she wanted more and worked with much vigor to keep up with his rough galloping stride. Suddenly the fury was gone. Chad's rage had faltered, leaving her still wanting more.

"Come on. Why are you stopping," she whispered? "What's wrong?" she still churned out energy, strokes after a stroke, but to no avail. His steel rod had quickly melted and backed out at a snail's pace.

"Damn, see what you made me do," Chad said, "that pussy is too tight, shit made me come too fast."

"What do you mean I made you come too fast?" the young, inexperienced Tabora asked, "I'm ready now . . . wait don't go, shoot. You mean that's it? You're just gonna leave me here?" she cried. "What about me?" The sudden cold air between her legs made her know that it was over, but would he be back, she wondered?

"Oh, what about you, huh? Slow your roll, I'll be back," said Chad. He grabbed a hand full of his clothes and walked out of the room. He left Tabora's hungry body to lay alone in the dark, screaming for just a moment of ecstacy; her torso twitched up and down with burning desires locked inside, between her legs, and she hoped he hurried back. She rubbed both her inner thighs and was about to massage –

The door finally opened again, she got excited, then immediately turned and saw that the silhouette was that of Baby Chris. Her mind instantly objected, but those objections were quickly over ruled by her body's desires, so she laid quiet and still while she watched him undress and don a rubber. She closed her eyes. Baby Chris made his way toward her, then inside of her. Baby Chris allowed her the opportunity to come while in the arms of a man; she lay beneath him pleased, yet vigorous; she wanted more.

"Where are you going?" She asked Chris, who had already got his, and didn't bother answering her.

This was a lot more than she'd bargained for but there was no need protesting, she wanted her fill for the first time in her life. So, while Baby Chris grabbed his clothes she prepared her body and mind for what she knew was to come.

It stood to reason that the train wouldn't end there with Baby Chris. Danny was in tow and followed closely behind him.

"Damn, sweetheart, where the hell are you?" he whispered.

"Shush," she said softly and closed her eyes after she saw Danny feeling his way over to her.

Both Danny and Baby Chris could have found their way over to the bed blind folded if they needed to, they had found the bed with other girls lying in it countless times before Tabora.

Danny too, taught the young Tabora something that she had only heard of before then, and he told her that it was called Doggie style, and yes, she adapted to his moves instantly. He pushed and pulled her waist with every stroke while she battled back his fury. "Ugh, ugh, ugh." Sweat poured from both of them. Tabora looked back over her right shoulder. She licked her lips and whipped the shine of sweat from her brow. She thought she saw Danny's eyes closed and knew there was a ways to go yet. She lowered her head between both her arms on the bed and stroked Danny until she heard his moaning and felt his thrust, his release.

* * *

A month had passed since Tabora's first sexual experience, and as crude as it may have seemed to others, it was a night she would cherish and remember always; she'd convinced herself that she was only seeking sex that night, not love or romance, and Tabora was okay with what went on that night at Chad's place. After some thought, she reasoned she'd satisfied her body's overbearing desires in the end, but only after having three men inside of her doggedly crushing her needs into submission.

Through it all, her first experience did not leave her disillusioned. In stead, she viewed it as a necessary means to an end, and could happen each time she sought pleasure. When she thought about it; all three men had their way with her; they each pumped her as would a pack of stray dogs on a bitch, and she loved it, one mount after the other. If there was one thing that she had to dislike about the experience, it would be the way all three men jumped up and ran out on her, perfectly willing to leave her unsatisfied if by chance she hadn't reached hers.

But nothing angered her more, however, than the scene Chad made just last night when she arrived at his apartment unannounced; his girl friend was there. He all but kicked her out of the building, but had the audacity to tell her: "call me later, but not tonight," he said.

She felt more disappointed than hurt because she viewed Chad as a sex partner after that first night, and one that she could count on when in need. But there he was with another woman, and calling her his girl.

Still, as a result of sheer desperation, she left Chad's apartment and finally got the sex she needed. She'd traveled to a Hotel bar on Allentown Road, near Andrews Air Force Base, just minutes from her home, and allowed herself to be picked up. And the experience was not bad at all, as she remembers it, after all, she practically grabbed the guy and led him out of the place.

More important, that experience made her realize that she was going to need a man all her own; a man capable of keeping up with her sexually, and not find faults with her healthy sexual desires.

As she sat and waited, she thought how High School was over now, and her full life was set to begin. She knew that it was time to find her place within society as a young woman managing a secret trove of highly charged sexual cravings, and what could be a life time of clandestine sexual behavior. No one can know about her challenges, she thought, especially Sara, and her parents.

Tabora didn't stop to give any thought to the many dangerous situations that may lay ahead, while she moved through shadows fulfilling her needs. All she could think about now was her friend Sara, who would soon be leaving her.

High up on the steps of a favorite spot of hers and Sara in Washington, D.C., the Lincoln Memorial, Tabora waited for Sara to arrive. This may be their last meeting for a while, Sara planned to go away to college shortly.

Tabora had not waited long before she observed Sara. . . . "What's that girl doing with some man?" Tabora murmured. Sara still climbed the steps when Tabora was able to get a good look at Sara and the man accompanying her. "Ulm?" Tabora rose to her feet and stretched; it was something she did to show off her physical assets. Both her arms extended above and behind her head; she arched her back ever so slightly. Her perfectly curved butt gave life to her tightly fitted blue jeans, while her breast demanded the attention she received from tourist and just plain passers–by alike, at the memorial.

"Damn, Sara," the man with her said, "is that your friend?"

Sara was well within Tabora's hearing range when she answered. "Yeah," she said, "that's my slut for a friend," she said jokingly. "Hey, girl, look at you, looking good enough to eat." Sara said. She smiled lustfully while admiring Tabora's anatomy as much as the man with her did.

Tabora, though, didn't catch the subtle hint of Sara's admiration, instead, as in high school, she was too busy defending her secret sexual shortcomings.

"Girl, you know that I heard you, and I'm no slut," Tabora replied, looking side ways at the stranger. "At least I'm by my self, but I can't say the same for you."

She noticed the strange look on Sara's face just before she spoke. "Tabora, you've never met my cousin, Omar?"

Oh no wonder, and that explains the look she gave me. Her cousin, huh, damn he's fine, she concluded silently.

"No, I've never met Tabora," Omar interjected. The twinkle in his eyes spoke volumes for the deep-rooted intentions that sparked his eager response, and Tabora read them well; her eyes swept downward to his crotch then back up to meet his. She liked him, and wanted him to know it.

"Tabora, this is my cousin Omar. Omar, this is Tabora. Remember I told you I had a cousin who had completed law school some time ago?"

"Yeah, I remember that," Tabora said, "So Omar how are you doing?" Tabora stepped down one step and embraced Omar firmly against her breast. He seemed several years older than she was, but to the young sexually wounded Tabora, he was hot. "Mm, Okay than," Tabora said near enough to Omar's ear for him to hear her, and feel her soft lips against his ear; she felt his reaction against her leg, and knew then that he wanted her as much as she wanted him.

"So, are you headed off to school too, Tabora?" Omar asked while enjoying the moment. He smoothed her upper back with his right hand before it slid to the lower portion of her back, then around her firm waist line.

Tabora stepped back from their embrace slowly, and threw her head back to realign her wind-blown hair. While her head was back, her eyes swept back and across to Omar. She caught the stare that his dreaming eyes gave her body. She blushed, then replied.

"No, not just yet anyway," she said. "But I certainly will miss my girl."

"Omar, this girl needs a job," Sara said, "is there something she can do at the law firm where you are? What's the name of it again?"

Omar smiled. "It's called, Dunn, Hope, Jasper&Brown," Omar said, "I've only been there one year myself, but I'll be happy to look into it for you, if you'd like me to."

"Sure, I'd love that, do you need my phone number or anything?" Tabora waited to recite her phone number into his cell phone when Omar reached into his pocket and handed her one of his cards. "No need, just hang-on to this card," he said, "and you can call me at the office anytime, Tabora." Tabora liked how Omar didn't jump all over her phone number, and began to wonder just how he might be in bed. They stood smiling at each other –

"Now that's my girl right there cousin and miss thang, that's my cousin, so you two have to keep it real with each other." Sara said. Sara stepped in front of Tabora and gave her a warm embrace.

"I'm really going to miss you girl," she said.

"Damn, I know you're leaving and all, but you don't need to be all up in me like that," Tabora said, jokingly, and broke away from Sara's seemingly overly warm embrace. She saw the puzzled look on Sara's face, but paid it no mind; she thought she'd hurt Sara's feelings, but she would have to deal with that later.

Tabora stepped back nearer to Omar and glanced at how his telling eyes danced up and down her body, and quickly forgot Sara's expression.

"I'm old enough to handle this situation professionally Lil cousin. Tabora will be all right, won't you Tabora?"

With her back now to Omar, and facing Sara, Tabora crossed her right leg tightly in front of her left leg where she stood on the step, with her butt almost against Omar's bulging crotch.

"Sure, I'll be fine in Omar's care, I'm sure of it," she said.

Sara finally left for college, and Omar was true to his word. He'd managed to get Tabora a job at the law firm where he worked, and the two of them saw each other regularly. The months went by, and Tabora had to grow up fast. Considering how close she and Omar had become, the older Omar wanted to maintain a clean professional appearance on the job. "Don't hang around my office or try to carry on small talk when we're at work," he would say to her. And then there were times when he told her: "its no one's business at the office that we know each other well, so you need to maintain a level of professionalism on the job."

Tabora finally adhered to Omar's sound advise, and settled in on the job. She learned to carry herself like the professional that he thought she should be on the job, and it all began to work out for her. She wanted nothing more than for it to work out for her, and hoped that the relationship they'd established would stay on course also.

3

"Ugh, ugh, ugh, c' mon, Omar . . . you can't keep up with this, or what?" Tabora said. She was in a doggie position with Omar, who in an attempt to make Tabora spill her juices once again as she so gallantly strived for; his slow churn was no match for her output of in and out thrusts. She turned and looked over her right shoulder. "Damn, Omar, is it going down? Don't tell me you're doing that shit to me again," she moaned.

"Girl, look, I can't keep this kind of shit up with you. I've been non stop screwing your ass on a regular for what, eighteen months now? Girl I have other duties now, and you know it." Omar said.

Tabora knew right away that his other duties referred to his relationship with his fiancee, Janet.

"Shit, I guest I'll have to be replacing your old ass," Tabora said, jokingly.

Omar facial expressions changed. He leaned back, pushed off his knees and rested his back against the king size head board at the end of the bed.

"Damn old man, I was just joking," Tabora said. Omar appeared hurt by her last remark, and she felt sort of bad for saying it. But it turned out that nothing could have been further from the truth. Omar, it seemed, had other things on his mind.

"Remember when we started seeing each other and I told you I had a girl? Anyway, Janet and I are getting married pretty soon, so you and I are going to have to stop our situation we have here, you know, for a little while anyway. I need to start having something left when I get home, and babe you have a way of draining a brother dry," Omar said with a somber look on his face.

"What, motha fucka?" Tabora jumped to her feet. Sweaty and winded, her brown skin shone against the lights in the downtown hotel room. She still had the body of a seventeen-year-old, and she knew it, but right now she didn't give a shit about that.

And yes, she knew about his woman from the beginning, but somehow was led to believe that she could win him over in bed, where her best asset lay, but no. She stared at his sweaty, muscular ass and could not believe what the low down bastard was telling her; he did not want anything more to do with her good pussy, her head jobs, and all the other freaky things she'd brought into his life. She was 'pissed', and had reason to be; he'd complained to her many times in the past about how Janet did not make him feel in bed the way she did, and that spawned false hopes of being able to have him all to herself some day. Now this, hell no, she wasn't having it?

"You come here today knowing damn well you were going to tell me that shit, yet your no–screwing ass put your little dick in me before you decided to tell me? Fuck you Omar."

"Look, there's no need for name calling," Omar said seemingly trying to be civil. "We've still got to work together and we've got to still keep whatever our relationship end up being, professional on the job."

"You know what. Get your old tired ass out of my sight," Tabora shouted.

Omar scowled and rushed to the other side of the bed where Tabora watched with anxious uncertainty, she had already suffered through periods of Omar's violent rages; he'd slapped her around a few times in the past, and convinced her that she'd made him do it. This time, however, he grabbed and squeezed her face with his right hand.

"Look 'ho," he growled in no uncertain terms, "you'd better stay in your place or you'll find my foot planted in that pretty little ass of yours." Omar grinned. He looked down at her naked butt before he smacked her with his left hand on the right cheek of her butt. "Am I getting through to you?"

"Yes," she replied, "I hear you." Angry but aware of Omar's tendencies to lay hands on her, Tabora stared into his eye in complete silence.

Omar pushed her naked body onto the bed. "You're a nobody, and you best remember that shit. Look at you."

He dressed himself quickly, and tucked his shirt into his pants, straightened his collar, then he walked to the door.

"Get dressed and get your ass out of here," he said, "I'll deal with you later." He slammed the door behind him.

"Fuck you, Omar," Tabora shouted. She cried. "Damn men," she murmured, "All of them are as lame as shit."

That was not Omar's first time jumping her bones like the dog that she knew him to be, and Tabora was tired of it, but she never wanted to upset him by breaking the seemingly promising relationship that they had sustained for such a long time; after the little stunt he'd just pulled, however, she cared less about his feelings. In addition, Mr. Dunn, who was among the most seniors of partners at the law firm where she and Omar worked, had been trying to woo her for some time now, and maybe it was time she started giving in to his pursuits.

"Yeah," she murmured, "that's what I'll do." She stared at the door deviously. "Mr. Omar Johnson, you won't have me to worry with much longer." She murmured. Tabora took her time and freshened up before taking the short walk back to work.

In a much better mood since she'd decided on a means of payback on Omar, Tabora had her swagger back. As she strolled back to the office smiling with yellow sun rays against the smooth skin of her radiant face, Tabora knew that it was her time to use what she's got to get the things she wanted from men for a change. "Yeah, I'm going to get mine," she murmured.

Tabora's eagerness to trump Omar's position at the law firm and cause him grief, may cause her more grief and pain then it's worth, and she hadn't taken the time to give any thought to the volatile situations she could find herself involved in while attempting to play a game that she had no experience in at all.

4

"No, I told you my boys were coming over to discuss some business, and your ass would have to leave when they came." Chad said.

"I know, I just wish I could stay a little longer that's all, you know, so I could just eat you all up," Tabora responded. But she'd known Chad long enough to know that he was serious, and she had to go; she dressed quickly and was escorted out of the bedroom.

When he walked her through the living room, Baby Chris and Danny stopped talking long enough to speak.

"Hey Boo-Boo, how you doing baby girl," Danny asked.

"Hey, what's up, Tabora," said Chris, nonchalantly.

"Hi fellas," Tabora said. "I don't know what it is you all are up to, but you'd better be careful," she concluded.

"Yeah, yeah, see you later, girl," Chad said, pushing her out through the doorway.

Chad closed the door after letting her out, and turned to his loud talking friends.

"Man, I could hear you dudes from the back room, and it sounds to me like yawl might be trying to punk out on the hit," Chad said. "Check it out, if we do this one last job I know we can walk out of there with the kind of cash that can last us a while."

Chad was commonly known on the streets as Millhouse, because he wore eye glasses like the cartoon character. But that was where the resemblance stopped. If there was such a thing as a natural born street hustler, Millhouse would've served as the undisputed poster child. He was a high school drop out, and the hustle became the only thing he knew to do.

Millhouse and the 'fellas' were at his place trying to determine which job they would take on as their next big score.

"All that's good and all," Baby Chris responded, "my question to you is: is it safer to do another bank as oppose to taking down Big Kelly's drop house, sitting out there waiting to be hit?"

Baby Chris, quiet, yet dangerously lethal, but unlike his two partners, he had a conscious, and his compassion showed at times. He never was 100 percent committed to the thug life, though he benefitted dearly from his time on the streets; he'd made the money, and intellectually, he was quite capable of moving onto the next level with his cash. He'd aired his opinion knowing that he was always out voted by Millhouse and Danny when it came to selecting the jobs they would take on, and he had no reason to believe that this time would be different.

"The way I see it, brah," Danny said, "This bank shit is too easy to let go, and plus tomorrow is Friday, there will be plenty of 'jack' in them tellers drawers. So what I' d say to that is, why not do both the hits tomorrow, what the fuck, hah?"

Danny, a.k.a., Doo-Dirty, was the meanest of the three childhood friends, but lately he'd been one happy fella, and with the cash from their prior bank jobs, he had every reason to be. Announcing that the gang should take down two hits in one day was an example of Doo-Dirty's bodacious mentality as of late, and Doo-Dirty's brash tenacity certainly reflected that of the others in the young brazen gang.

The young gang members were riding high and enjoying the cash from many successful robberies of Washington, D.C. area banks, to include Maryland and Virginia, and apparently felt justified in believing that they were unstoppable; Danny's aggressive plan to pop two major scores in a single day certainly seemed to attest to their daring ways. What it meant, however, was that the bank job had to be flawless if the second hit was to take place at all.

Millhouse stood quietly at first, his eyes gleamed with joy through his glasses as he assessed the potential wind fall of cash from the two jobs combined.

"Damn, son, check you out boy, that's not bad at all . . . I'm down with that idea," said Millhouse.

"Yeah, I should have known, you two jokers always agree on shit, but I'm down," Baby Chris said, then he made an announcement neither of his two partners had expected from him.

"Look here, brah, after tomorrow, man, I'm not doing any more bank jobs, shit's too risky for me, man."

"What, are you sure about that? I mean, if you are, don't come begging for cash once your little change is gone, you know?" Doo-Dirty said, in no uncertain terms. Yet he hoped his long time friend would change his mind and decide to stay.

"I'm not worried about that shit, man. I told you I'm putting my cash into some legal shit, yo," Baby Chris explained" –

"Awe, man, you're serious about letting that 'ho from high school, what's her name?" Millhouse asked.

Doo-Dirty and Millhouse laughed loud and hard, the nerve of Baby Chris to think that some chick from his high school days was going to invest his dirty money, and somehow put him on the fast track to high social standings.

Millhouse found it hard to believe that Baby Chris was serious about that stupid shit, but he for one was tired of trying to talk him out of it; deep down, he knew that Baby Chris was different from him and Doo-Dirty, and felt he should break away from the hustle before it was too late.

"Janet Watts," Baby Chris said, "Her last name is Johnson now and she won't rip me off if that's where you're going with the shit. She does that for a living, and yeah I trust her."

"Okay, man, after tonight, Big Ed is gonna be riding with us." Millhouse explained. "So I hope your ass can stand behind that silly ass idea later on, when your cash is gone."

"That's cool, man, and I understand," Baby Chris said. "Another thing though, no damn drinking this time Doo-Dirty, though we managed the last time, you made it over to that security guard a little too late for comfort behind that drinking . . . I'll see you jokers tomorrow. Oh wait. We need to hookup tonight and take a couple of dry runs at Big Kelly's place."

"Yeah, okay, righteous one," Millhouse responded.

"Just don't be all night gettin' here, boy." Doo-Dirty shouted as Chris prepared to leave.

Baby Chris turned and walked out of the door. He could not help but think about his two friends, and how quickly they'd changed the gang's original plan. He remembers how in the beginning they all had agreed on attempting only a couple of bank robberies, but now they seemed to have planned a bank for every month this year, he thought, and smiled to himself. The hits no longer seemed like a means for making money as it was in the beginning, instead, it was more like they continued doing it for the love of the challenge, especially Doo-Dirty; he treated it as if it was as easy as taking a piss, Baby Chris reasoned.

The three of them had been there for each other through every type of drug deal, drug scam, robbery, and many other unsavory predicaments since high school. Now, with talk of bringing in Ezzard, a.k.a. Big Ed, things in the gang were definitely in for a change because Big Ed was a real live shooter, a hit man, and now they expect him to settle down and do bank robberies, Baby Chris thought not.

Baby Chris had found him a girl as well as a financial advisor when he found Janet, though she was married, and she hadn't slept with him yet, he felt he could count on her. Her husband, some punk ass lawyer, dogged her out every chance he got, but for whatever reason, she didn't want to leave him. Chris didn't complain about the arrangement between them at all, because she was to be more than just a piece of ass, she helped him to see new beginnings for himself, new ways of living a good clean life.

Being with Janet was different, and she eventually showed Baby Chris how he could get more out life than he'd ever been made to believe he could achieve, and all he had to do was walk away from the hustle. But he had been in the street game for most of his young life, and no one had ever told him that when the notion to walk away from the hustle hits you, simply go with it. Baby Chris had gradually worked himself to the point where he was able to face his partners and tell them of his plans to move onto something better in life, and he would use the money made from the hustle to take him there. But he had committed himself to two more jobs before leaving, and he had no idea how either job, nor his future, would turn out. One thing was certain: he didn't want this bank job to be like the last one they'd been on.

He thought about how Doo Dirty had taken a couple of drinks before they'd left for the hit, and that made for a sloppy entrance into the bank. Though Doo Dirty managed to get himself together in enough time to contain the security guard, and the job inside the bank went off all right. However, leaving the bank became even more life threatening for all of them, when no one saw the police cruiser when it pulled up and parked across the street from the bank that they were robbing. Doo Dirty spotted them on his way out, and pulled his weapon. Before Baby Chris or Millhouse knew what was going on, a shoot out had begun and Doo Dirty had already taken down one of the cops. How they got away is still a question that Chris asks himself to this day.

Those two cops must have been totally unaware of the bank robbery taking place across the street from them, because the shoot out seemed to frighten them out of their wits, Chris thought. Now after shooting the cop, they all know that the heat is on them now, and every cop in the tri-state area is hoping that they hit a bank in their town. Baby Chris shook his head while walking to his car. "Man. These are going to be my last two jobs," he muttered.

* * *

Tabora was away from her desk when Sara walked into the lobby of the law firm. She decided to be seated and wait near Tabora's desk until she returned. Tabora came from the left side hall way with her head down, she looked up at the visitor seated in the waiting area, and she did a quick double take.

"Girl!" she screamed and ran to Sara. "What are you doing here?"

Tabora embraced Sara in the center of the lobby, and the two of them seemed inseparable momentarily, thanks to the firm hold Sara had on her. Sara leaned back and fluffed Tabora's hair and smiled, then leaned in and kissed Tabora on her mouth.

"I've missed you so much," she said.

"Well, I guest you have," Tabora said, licking her lips. She wondered what was the idea behind the lip lock. Maybe it was one of those things Sara had picked up while away attending college? Tabora would not allow herself to put too much time into thinking about it. Her girl was home, and she was happy.

"How much longer will you be in town?"

"Until tomorrow at the latest. I'm going to meet a friend's dad and stay down there in Virginia with them a couple of days, or maybe the week," Sara replied.

"You look different, girl. Your hair is cut all low and everything. So when do I get to meet this friend of yours? Is he tall dark and handsome like we always talked about?"

"No ho, like you always talked about, remember?" Sara said. "And he is a she, just so you'll know."

"She?" Tabora said.

Just then the lobby door opened, and Tabora was thinking the worst about Sara, but hoped that she was wrong about her girl; the really short manly hair cut, and the lip lock gave credence to her thoughts. And when Tabora saw the young girl enter into the lobby, she unconsciously wiped her lips with the back of her right hand, and waited for formal introductions.

Sara looked and smiled as the young lady walked in and stood next to her.

"Tabora I'd like you to meet Taylor, and Taylor this is Tabora."

"I'm pleased to meet you, Taylor." Tabora said with a huge smile on her face. She extended her hand, but to no avail.

"I'm sure," Taylor replied, she gawked momentarily, then Taylor immediately turned to Sara. "You didn't tell me you were going to meet with her. Is this Tabora you told me so much about?"

"Wait, what is going on here?" Tabora said, scowling, then railed. It was bad enough the hussy didn't shake her hand, now this. "Does this bitch have a problem with me, or something?" Tabora asked.

"Tabora, wait a minute, just slow your roll," Sara said.

"No, you need to talk to Ms Thang here, not me."

"Okay then, we'll just go ahead and speak to Omar, because this isn't cutting it. I'll see you around."

Tabora stepped back and stared, and was surprised by Sara's actions. She dropped her head slightly and stared under eyed at Sara and Taylor, as they walked away hand in hand. "Sara?" she muttered, then smirked before placing the tip of her index finger between her lips, in thought; she had never considered the possibility of having sex with another woman, let alone Sara, but the thought made her body tingle all over.

Sara seemed to think that it was better to leave the lobby and visit Omar than to stay there by Tabora and have to put up with Taylor's insane jealousy. Sara had been a witness to Taylor's jealous tantrums while talking to a female classmate on campus; Taylor had to be escorted back to her dorm room until she had settled down. Sara knows that she's insecure and tries not to give too much of her attention to anyone else when she's with Taylor, and that was just to keep trouble down; she hoped Tabora would not be upset with her for leaving, or for her sexual preference.

Tabora couldn't believe what she'd seen with her own eyes, and began to think back over the years when they were both in grade school. Ms sacred pussy Sara, it seemed, had good reason for not chasing boys, Tabora reasoned, and yet she always got angry when Tabora did so; she should have known from the beginning that Sara was keeping something from her. Suddenly Tabora thought back to the question Taylor asked, and wondered just what in hell did Sara tell Taylor about the two of them? She returned to her desk, but they were not going to get anymore work out of her for the remainder of that day. "I'm just too through," she murmured, about Sara and her girl friend Taylor.

* * *

It was eleven a.m. when Baby Chris entered the bank and stood on line at the commercial accounts window. He waited anxiously with an empty tan tool bag strapped across his right shoulder until a bank worker opened the main door leading to the back hallway. It was common to stop any of the tellers when they headed to the back through that door, and ask questions about a transaction. So when Baby Chris did so it didn't raise any eye brows where the other customers were concerned. In addition, loud music from the small compact disk player on the right side of the bank's lobby drowned out Baby Chris' demands as he whispered them to the teller.

"Excuse me, Miss," Baby Chris said, as he moved quickly toward her. Before the teller could say anything, Chris had aggressively worked his way inside the door, out of sight of every one of the unsuspecting patrons standing in line, and the unsuspecting guard had just walked back into the bank from outside.

Once behind the closed door, and amidst the fast paced action, Chris pulled his scarf up from around his neck and covered the lower portion of his face. The teller spotted Chris' weapon. "Go ahead, open it. C' mon, get it open. Go," Chris said.

"Oh please, don't shoot, please," the frightened bank teller cried. Her hands trembled and caused her to miss the combination to the door leading to the tellers bay on several tries.

"You'd better get this door opened," Baby Chris growled. "Now."

Millhouse stood in the outer lobby, just inside of the double doorway leading into the bank. Through the plexiglass window, he could see the door leading to the tellers' work station when it finally opened. He stormed into the customer's lobby alone as planned.

"Everybody, get down . . . now!" Millhouse shouted. "You heard me nigga, get your fucking ass down."

One elderly customer nervously danced around and appeared unsure of what to do.

"Let's go, pops, get your old ass down on the floor too."

The security guard seemed confused at first, then carefully made a move for his weapon. "Let me have that pistol, my man." Doo-Dirty whispered from behind the security guard. The guard had eased his pistol out of its holster in an apparent attempt to shoot Millhouse, who's back was to him. Millhouse had purposely run pass the guard upon entering the bank's lobby, as part of the plan. It was a dangerous move on Millhouse's part that relied on Doo-Dirty being in place promptly to relieve the guard of his weapon; Millhouse looked over and gave Doo-Dirty apparent eyes of approval for a job well done.

Baby Chris glanced at the two of them from his position behind the tellers' plexiglass window; he didn't like the unnecessary careless antics of his two friends, it could only lead to trouble for them someday, and he didn't want to be around when that day came. He quickly turned his attention back toward the tellers, who nervously filled sacks of cash.

"Let's go people," Baby Chris shouted, "empty those drawers into the bag and pass it down. If I think I see a dye cannister, two of you will die instantly. Baby Chris was stern and believable; all the tellers complied. "Keep those feet and hands where I can see" –

"Let's go, let's go," shouted Millhouse from the lobby. He pushed his glasses higher on the bridge of his nose.

Baby Chris' moves were quick and calculated as he exited the teller's area, behind the one inch thick plexiglass security window. He had the tan suede tool bag with bills of all denominations inside. He ran to the hallway door to the customer lobby, exited and ran passed Millhouse and Doo-Dirty, who still manned their positions. Outside, where he casually walked to the van parked along the side of the bank; he waited anxiously for Millhouse and Doo-Dirty. Millhouse walked briskly around the corner to the waiting van. He pushed up on his glasses and took a quick look behind him. Doo-Dirty came around the building running, his weapon still visible when he fell to the ground causing a scene momentarily. He quickly recovered and ran to the van laughing.

"What? What? Doo-Dirty shouted, "yeah, I told you that shit, man. Didn't the shit go just like I said it would?

"Damn son, please, relax," Baby Chris replied. "Why is it we have to hear your mouth every time your bragging ass bring a job to the table that works?"

"Damn, don't you two start that arguing and shit just yet," said Millhouse as his eyes swept the highway behind them in search of any unwanted guest. "We've got to get rid of this hot ass van at the mall before we celebrate, okay?" There was momentary silence as the van roared along the planned escape route, but Baby Chris knew that it wouldn't last.

"That shit did go like clock work, though, my nigga," Millhouse finally admitted. He turned to the back seat to give Doo-Dirty a solid high five.

"That figures, you two jokers sticking together as usual." Baby Chris said. "And you need to fix your glasses, Millhouse." They all laughed.

The men laid low at Millhouse's apartment after they drove the van to the old Landover Mall parking lot and picked up their car as planned. They celebrated lightly while they went over the plans for the hit on Big Kelly's drop house that was set for later that night. Baby Chris wanted everything to go well later tonight; if it didn't, he knew he would never hear the end of it from Doo-Dirty, who was riding high after this morning's job on the bank; Chris had provided the information for the drop house robbery, and all four men had spent ample time observing the place on several dry runs they had taken late last night; Millhouse decided to take Big Ed along to get his feet wet.

Baby Chris barely knew Big Kelly, who he met through another friend during a drug transaction, but the more he learned about Big Kelly's organization and his net worth, the more he quietly snooped around. He was able to find out about the drop house from talkative insiders among Kelly's crew. If what he'd heard was true about the large sums of cash and drugs located at the drop house, he knew for sure that this would be his last hustle, and no more taking unnecessary chances just for the sport of it, like Millhouse and Doo-Dirty.

He sat across the room and watched as they celebrated, and thought about how sad it was that he couldn't talk them into giving up the dumb shit also, before their luck ran out.

"Come on boy, what are you sitting over there looking at, let's drink one beer, at least." Doo-Dirty said."

"Yeah, what the hell, huh?" said Baby Chris. He joined them in the one drink.

* * *

It was eleven thirty p.m., in the Upper Marlboro, Maryland suburb, in what looked like some sort of dark countryside. Thick trees and brush lined both sides of the single lane winding road that led to Big Kelly's drop house; the turnoff road that led directly to the house was even narrower, a dirt road. There were two boarded houses, one on each side of the dirt road that led directly in front of Big Kelly's place and ended in a dust-filled turn around, a cal-de-sac. The openings in the trees along the dirt road and the opening around the property were the only places, it seemed, that was moonlit.

The fact that the men did dry runs during the night had paid off already; they had no trouble finding the place. The van drove one block pass the two houses and parked along the shoulder of the dirt road facing the drop house. The driver they brought along, Big Ed, was to wait until the three men were inside of the house to drive the van up the one hundred yards to the house and 'post–up' on the side door; according to Baby Chris' information, the side door was the only other exit other than the front door; the other windows and doors were all boarded.

Baby Chris stood at the hood of the van going over some last minute details with Millhouse and Doo Dirty before launching their assault on Big Kelly's unsuspecting gang inside. They could hear ladies' voices inside over the loud music. To Baby Chris' surprise, the three men inside tasked with protecting the place had apparently compromised their own security when they invited the women over, and seemed to be showing them a good time. That was a big plus for the men outside, in more ways than one. The woman's presence meant that the security dogs that Chris had heard so much about must be put away in one of the back rooms of the house, he reasoned.

The two cars along the side of the house, just forward of the side door, must belong to the gang members inside, Baby Chris thought. He asked Millhouse to tip up to the house alone, and get a better look at who might be inside. The music inside had to be loud because it all but shook the rafters outside.

"Damn, them boys are having themselves a good time in that joint," Millhouse murmured before returning to Chris' and Doo Dirty's location. "You boys ready, man?" Millhouse asked. "Those niggas are in side freaking and shit, this should be better than we figured."

"Shit yeah, let's do this shit, man," Doo Dirty replied. "You're not gettin' no weak stomach or no shit like that or you, Chris?"

"No, motha fucka, I'm cool, but let's see how your ass make out if the lead starts flying."

"A'ight, let's move in on those clowns." Millhouse said. He pushed his glasses up firmly on the bridge of his nose "Yawl can finish that shit when this is over, okay?"

* * *

Big Kelly was upstairs in his Bowie, Maryland home, and in the middle of celebrating in advance of the biggest drug deal he was to ever take part in. He had worked long and hard for his white collar, Washington, D.C. drug connection, and had finally earned their trust; he would soon partake in his organization's largest drug transaction to date. The drugs were in place and under the watchful eye of his trusted men. Between them and his two highly trained dogs on duty at his Upper Marlboro drop house, he was certain that everything would be okay. All he awaited now was tomorrow's meeting with the couriers from out of town.

"Hold on girl. The shit ain't going anywhere. Now slow your roll," he said to Tonya, who greedily sniffed lines of cocain from his chest, then rushed to reach the lines near his thighs. No sooner then she reached his thighs the phone rang.

"Don't stop sweetheart," he said as he leaned over carefully and grabbed the receiver.

"You got me, now spill it," he said, filled with frustrations.

"Is everything on that end ready for tomorrow?" the low, muffled voice asked.

"Oh, shit. Mr. J," he said. Big Kelly pushed Tonya's head away from his penis and slid up against the head board. "Yes Mr. J everything is set and ready to go."

"These are very dear friends of mine, and a lot is at stake here, so don't blow this. I know you said that your place was secured, but I want you to send a couple more men out there just in case." Mr. J. said.

"Sure, I'll do it right away, Mr. J."

"Do it now." Mr. J's voice rippled with intensity, causing Big Kelly's head to flinch away from the receiver.

"I'll get" –

The phone went dead as Mr. J. hung up on Big Kelly.

"Who was that honey?" Tonya asked, sniffing hard through her nostrils and looking up at him.

"What, bitch the only business you have in this joint is between my legs, now get here and handle yours." Big Kelly barked. He leaned back against the head board of the bed, closed his eyes while his huge legs parted. "Nosy ass motha fucka," he murmured, then moaned "um, mm, shit."

There was no doubt Tonya knew her business; she started at his ankle and worked her way up to his hard pulsating dick. She worked Big Kelly into a frenzy with the things she did to him. Each time he reached for her head, she pushed his hands away.

"Oh, hh, bitch. That fucking mouth of yours is the shit. Ugh, shit, ho. I love you," Big Kelly cried.

As it turned out, in the heat of the moment Big Kelly lost touch with his own business priorities and neglected to follow strict orders from his boss. He failed to send more men out to the drop house as extra security for multimillion dollars worth of drugs he'd been entrusted with holding and delivering.

* * *

The three men appeared as silhouettes against the moon lit night, as they moved through the wide opened area that led directly to the house.

All three men eased up to the front door with caution. Millhouse gave Doo-Dirty and Chris the thumbs up then stepped back and savagely displayed the awesome strength of his right leg. He kicked the solid wood door. It sprung opened breaking the wood door jamb. Millhouse was bombarded by the loud music from inside. Caught by surprise, Big Kelly's men all jumped and seemed to quickly realize what they had allowed to happen, and none of them moved a muscle. Their lady friends, however, screamed almost as loud as the music.

Doo-Dirty and Baby Chris moved in, Chris looked around frantically for the stereo's receiver. He spotted it shortly after and took aim. Pop . . . pop. Everyone in the room jumped, to include Millhouse and Doo-Dirty, and except for the screams coming from the panicking women, the room was quiet.

"Okay boys, this is it," Millhouse shouted to the surprised occupants, then continued. "You boys got caught with your pants down, huh? Get your ass on the floor, all of you. Now."

All three partially nude women scurried to cover their bodies from the intruders while pleading for their lives.

"Shut your ass up 'ho." Millhouse shouted to the loudest of the women, but quieted all three; they too came to rest on the floor.

Though all three men remained calm and in control of the situation, there was no money or drugs any where in their sights; Baby Chris was concerned. To make matters worst, one of the three captives suddenly jumped up from the floor. He ran for the hallway toward the side door. Big Ed, doing as he was told kicked the side door in just as the fleeing man reached it. The door flew opened and smacked the runner in his face. Impact from the solid wood door knocked him backwards. He landed on his back. By then Doo-Dirty, who was in pursuit, grabbed him in his collar.

"Get your ass up boy. Try that shit again and you're dead." The dazed runner stumbled back to the living room where he rejoined his friends. Millhouse was relieved that they caught the bum because the last thing they wanted was to start shooting if they didn't have to. Big Ed entered at the side door and signaled to Baby Chris to cover him while he checked out the four rooms down the hallway that led toward the rear of the house.

Baby Chris looked on from where he stood in the living room, just at the beginning of the hallway. Big Ed had kicked in three of the doors and found nothing. He now stood in front of the last door at the end of the hallway.

"Hey man, what is Ed doing back there?" Millhouse asked, pushing up his glasses. "What about. . . ."

"Au shit," Baby Chris shouted, "Ed, don't kick that door" –

It was too late to stop Ed. He'd kicked the last door in. It was no wonder the windows and door on the back of the house were sealed, everything Baby Chris said would be in the house was there in the back room, money, garbage bags full of it, and drugs stacked high. Big Ed stood still in front of the door way, as if he'd seen a ghost, Baby Chris thought.

He could not move, or he did not want to move. He stood nervously staring at two beastly, muscle clad rottweiler dogs that stood in the center of the doorway; Big Kelly had both the dogs trained specifically for attack purposes, neither of them had ever seen any action. They both growled with hungry eyes while displaying their huge, pointed canines and a great deal of gums. The two animals were both better than one hundred pounds each in weight and wore matching spiked collars. Big Ed, who still had not moved a muscle, was afraid to cry out for help. Suddenly he noticed both dogs when they displayed the same savagery looks. They both growled in harmony as they swiftly made their moves to take action against the intruders.

It seemed Big Ed had no time at all to react to the dogs' fury; one of the dogs attacked him high. "Ooh, hh, sssshit," Big Ed yelled. The huge dog's impact knocked him backwards and to the floor. "Heeelp! Get this, ughh, help." Ed's screams for help consequently turned to screams of pain. He kicked, and screamed while lying on his back squirming from left to right. He had no thoughts of attempting to retrieve the weapon he'd dropped upon being attached. Instead, he began to punch the dog, and fight him like a man.

Doo-Dirty heard screams and looked away from the captives inside the living room. He rushed over to where Baby Chris stood. Chris appeared to be in shock; he just stood and watched the muscular beast as it and Big Ed fought. By the time he and Doo-Dirty realized that the other dog would bypass Ed, it was too late. The other beastly animal charged savagely down the hallway at full stride and headed straight in Doo-Dirty's and Baby Chris direction with grave intent. Both men stood idle, but only for a moment.

DooDirty wisely, but nervously turned his weapon on the fast charging beast, but to no avail. The game animal went airborne, landing paws first in the center of Baby Chris' chest. The animal seemed bigger than life, Baby Chris thought. The dog's momentum forced Baby Chris all the way back across the living room, and out of the busted front door. When Chris could no longer attempt to escape, the animal went to work quickly, and he ripped into Baby Chris' flesh. The more Chris fought, it seemed, the worst punishment he received; the dog dragged him like a rag doll before standing over Chris and shaking him about.

Frightened and surprised by the sudden attack, Baby Chris, shamelessly did what came natural

"Hhelp. Get this motha fucka off me, man."

He screamed like a bitch and knew it, but it was to be expected, and at that particular moment he didn't give a shit. "Dirty! Millhouse, c' mon, get him of me. Ouch, ugh, shit." Their male captors all stood with their hands in the air laughing at the attack, while the ladies screamed at the tops of their voices.

"Shut your asses, all of you," Doo-Dirty shouted, in a panic. "Let me hear another word and everybody dies in here."

Doo-Dirty reluctantly turn his attention away from his hostages again, but briefly. He stepped out of the door for a clear shot at the vicious animal atop Baby Chris. He looked back at the hostages, then back at Baby Chris. He had to do something quick. He stepped along the side of the dog and at point-blank range he fired. Pop.

Millhouse, who seemed caught between watching the hostages and seemingly wondering what else could possibly go wrong, heard the screams of Baby Chris on the front porch and Ed in the back hallway. His moves were slow but deliberate as he kept his gun pointed at the hostages and positioned himself to see Ed down the hallway. He took careful aim down the hallway and fired. Pop . . . pop. The dog's body went limp, and fell mostly onto Big Ed; Ed, still punching and screaming, finally pushed the huge hunk of bleeding flesh off him and raced for the side door. He jumped passed all the steps and onto the ground.

The one close range shot from Doo-Dirty did not kill the dog on the front porch. The dog screamed, looked to its left at Doo-Dirty as if it would attack, but instead, it turned to run. Doo-Dirty shot twice. Pop . . . pop. The dog staggered and fell to the ground, then reared up once again and ran directly into the wooded area at the end of the circled dirt road.

Millhouse turned his attention back to his hostages, only to learn that in the few seconds of distractions the prisoners had gamely reached their weapons. Millhouse fired his own weapon while he hurriedly ran for the front door opening. Gun shots erupted from the prisoners inside, then return fire came from outside of the house.

Millhouse returned fire, Doo-Dirty, in the midst of the action, ran over to the doorway and grabbed the injured Baby Chris, who struggled to clear himself from the line of fire. The women screamed louder as the thunderous sound of the guns firing echoed throughout the moon lit night.

Doo-Dirty sensed that the plan was out the window. "Shit, man, what the fuck went wrong in there? Those niggas are dug– in. Where the hell is. . . ."

Before Doo-Dirty could ask where Big Ed had gone, he rushed back into the side door firing his weapon like a mad man. He instantly took out two of the men inside from his position behind them, just inside the hallway.

Doo-Dirty and Millhouse, still positioned on the front porch, got the break they needed from Big Ed's actions; they fired into the house at will. Finally, after moments of being fired upon from both directions, the firing and screaming inside all came to a halt.

"Yeah, you bitches," Millhouse screamed, "c'mon man, we gotta do this shit quickly."

"I can't, man," Baby Chris moaned. He laid helpless on the porch.

Doo-Dirty, Millhouse and Big Ed, who was injured but able to walk, quickly checked the bodies inside, everyone to include the women were dead. "Damn, those 'hos was in the wrong place at the wrong time, what a waste," Ed said, favoring his left arm.

"Come on, man, stop fucking around," Doo-Dirty said, thinking that Baby Chris was joking. He and Ed joined Millhouse in the back room and they began loading much more drugs and money then they anticipated finding. Once the van was loaded and the men were ready to go, Millhouse and Doo-Dirty carried Baby Chris' badly injured body to the van where Ed waited to drive them out of the wooded area. Millhouse sat in the front seat after they loaded Baby Chris into the back along with Doo-Dirty and bags of cash and drugs. The van was quiet at first, but then Doo-Dirty finally broke the silence. And when he did, Baby Chris knew that it wouldn't be long after that he would have to hear Doo-Dirty's shit.

"Yeah, shit yeah," Doo-Dirty shouted, "that shit was all that and some." He laughed and fell back against his seat, and looked down at Baby Chris, who was slumped down next to him, and he laughed harder.

"I don't know Chris," Doo-Dirty said, "your crazy ass just gotta get mad with me on this one, brah, cause I can't help myself. . . .

"Nigga, you should've seen the look on your sorry ass face when that big, black ass dog grabbed hold of your screaming ass," Doo-Dirty reared backward and screamed. He laughed uncontrollably.

Baby Chris had just gotten his ass whipped fair and square by a dog, and didn't find the shit all that funny. He seemed ready to curse Doo-Dirty's ass out before he thought about it for a second or two. In the meantime, after seeing Doo-Dirty laughing so hard, he thought of how the shit could have been just a little funny, now that it was over, of course. "Man, fuck you, Danny," Baby Chris shouted. All three friends laughed loudly. Ed glanced through the rear view mirror at Baby Chris, and he too joined in the laughter, cautiously, as he slowly maneuvered the van along the dirt road and back to the main street.

"Man how do you think this, Big Kelly dude get his hand on so much powder?" Millhouse finally asked, after catching his breath and fixing his glasses.

"I don't know," said Doo-Dirty, "but the shit is all ours now. Ain't that right Chris?"

Baby Chris saw Big Ed laughing and wondered why Ed wasn't in as much pain as he was, and what the hell was he laughing at, the dog had kicked his ass too.

5

"I don't know, baby," Omar said, then leaned down to take a sip from his coffee cup, "you've handled investment accounts for some suspect investors before in the three years we've been married, but none of them ever came as close as this one to crossing the line."

"Well I knew Chris when I was in high school, though he was still in middle school then, we became good friends" –

"You needn't tell me any more about it, thank you," Omar said.

Janet looked strangely at Omar for his standoffish response, and was careful with her own; she had long since experience his womanizing ways, and didn't want to upset him.

"Don't even start with that, okay, Omar? Anyway, when Chris came to me he talked about having large sums of money. The situation actually could have gotten worst if I had accepted the lump sum of money that he initially brought to me," Janet explained, she seated herself at the kitchen counter next to Omar, "I ended up telling Chris to place a limited amount of cash into the account each quarter in order to circumvent the ridiculous law of having to turn him into the IRS. Because I know him, I have a good idea where his money comes from, but it's his business how he makes the money. Though it may not seem worth all the trouble now, in the end it will be a very large account that will pay me well."

"Good," Omar said, "as long as I don't have to end up representing you in court on criminal charges, okay?" Omar smiled then found himself staring down at Janet's silky redbone legs. She certainly was 'looking hot' sitting there discussing money. The subject alone seemed to turn her on. He only wished that he could be turned on by her in that way, maybe then he would succumb to her sexual needs more often; he'd been put off by Janet ever since she'd refused to 'freak' him in bed; he wanted her to do the things to him that Tabora and some of his other outside women were doing to him in bed, after all, he reasoned, she is his wife.

When he slept with Tabora on a regular basis behind Janet's back, Janet was all but pushed aside, he seldom had any love left in him when he would go home to her after screwing other women all day. She knew all the time what he was out doing when he claimed to be with clients, but she kept her damaging thoughts to herself. Truth is, she felt that their relationship had gotten better for a while, but then lately, she'd been getting the same bad treatment as she did once before, when he ran around on her a lot; lately it didn't seem to matter what she did to turn him on in bed. He turned her away, refusing to satisfy her needs.

He smirked as he watched her heart-shaped face with its dimpled smile.

"What?" she asked.

Omar didn't mind being in the position to refuse Janet whenever she tried to seduce him, but it didn't sit too well with him when she appeared to not be interested in him when he attempted to come onto her, and she knew that.

"Nothing, baby," Omar explained, he turned and placed his right hand firmly on her left thigh. "I was just checking you out, you know?"

Janet stared down at his hand, then he watched as she eyed him with disdain.

His clothes had stunk of cheap perfume these past couple of months and he never seemed to have had time to make love to her at all any more. She defiantly brushed his hand from her thigh. She rose from the maple wood stool.

"That's very considered of you to at least check me out," Janet said, then walked into the kitchen. "There's nothing wrong with me. You do know that, right? I'm a fine healthy black woman, you need to recognize my needs and stop running around with every little slut you come into contact with."

"What? What are you talking about now, woman?" Omar asked, then squirmed in his seat. "I don't have a game, and I'm being faithful to you, if that's what you mean. I come home to you every evening, same time, how can I possibly be having an affair?"

"You're certainly not loving me is all I know and that's a dangerous way to leave any woman. I have needs too you know."

"Look, let's discuss this matter later this evening, okay baby? I promise you it'll get better. I guess I have had some things from the office on my mind lately."

"Au huh, well, I've got to get ready to leave here myself," Janet said, then departed the kitchen to prepare herself for work. She hoped Omar would not follow her to the bed room. She did not want to be bothered with anymore of his lies. On and off for weeks now he had come home smelling like some cheap 'ho and not just his cloths, his whole body. "He must think I'm crazy," she muttered.

She walked by the full length mirror in the bedroom then stopped. She walked backward to the mirror. Janet slowly slid the straps of her silk gown from each of her shoulders and wiggled her body, slightly churning, to allow her silk gown to flow down from her body to the floor. She stared at her naked body in the mirror. While warmly caressing herself, Janet allowed both her hands to slowly glide down inside her thighs. "Ooh. Huh, his ass doesn't have to want this. I know that this is a worthy piece of ass, to say the least," she murmured. She closed her eyes. Two fingers of her left hand pierced the rounds of her pussy while her right hand slid up to her left nipple. She massaged it hard. "Oh, hh, shit," she moaned. She opened her eyes and rushed into the shower.

* * *

On the forth floor of the Executive Tower, in the law offices of, Dunn, Hope, Jasper, & Brown. An early morning meeting between the partners was well underway in the conference room. Their voices could be heard in the lobby outside of the conference room where the receptionist, Tabora was just about to be seated at her desk. The discussion grabbed and demanded Tabora's attention. However, she seemed guided by what had become her office professionalism; to avoid listening, she first tampered with the stapler, then the paper weight; Yet her ears nonetheless, tweaked with every passing word that flowed out of the conference room, and into the lobby where she sat. Finally, she stopped fumbling. Instead, she leaned shamelessly more to her left, toward the conference room. She smiled and listened.

"That's it then." Mr. Dunn said. He was one of the senior partners at the firm. Tabora recognized his voice when he spoke, she would know it any where.

"We've got ourselves a new counselor on one of the biggest cases this firm has had in a while. We'll make the announcement tomorrow." Mr. Dunn said.

"Well, if there's no more business to be settled, let's rap it up. Thanks again everyone for coming in so early to make this work. Heaven knows we needed the shouting time." Said Mr. Jasper.

The meeting was held early that morning to meet with the schedules of some of the senior partners, and also to keep the partners' business decisions from reaching the ears of the rest of the office's staff.

The partners began pouring out of the conference room into the lobby when one of them said. "I thought no one was to be here but us?" The partner noticed Tabora seated at her desk. She sat with a look of concern draping her face; she was personally asked to come in early by Mr. Dunn, and wondered what all the questions were about.

Meanwhile, inside the conference room, Mr. Jasper grabbed Mr. Dunn by his left arm and forced him to a nearby corner, and stared him down with discontentment.

"This is the second time you've influenced the decision of the others on cases important to this firm, I don't like it, and won't tolerate it again."

Mr. Dunn scowled and snatched his arm from the grasp of Mr. Jasper then fired back.

"You just deal with the garbage you call clients, and let me handle what goes on around this office."

"Look at you, you'll never be the man nor the attorney that your father was," Mr. Jasper said.

"Is that why my father ended up dying so mysteriously, Mr. J.?"

Mr. J. ignored Marc's last statement, as if he never spoke the words, and Marc was not the only one who felt that the older Mr. Dunn's death was suspicious; he was last seen with Mr. Jasper, but no charges were ever brought against him. "Your wife working nights at the hospital leaves you with too much time on your hands is all I'm saying."

"Just leave my wife out of this, and I handle my end of the business very well, thank you."

"Look, I told you that I thought Omar was the best person for the case and you did everything in your power to see that he didn't get it." Mr. Jasper stepped in closer to Mr. Dunn, then continued. "You need to start thinking with your head and not your dick, perhaps then the chips would begin to fall where they may around this office."

Mr. Dunn grinned, and had no response to the comment. He turned and hurried out to the lobby to see who it was the others were talking about.

"Tabora . . . au, Ms Thymes, what are you doing here this time of morning?" asked Mr. Dunn, looking around at his associates'.

"Sir, you asked me to come in to meet"–

"Oh yes, that. That was cancelled Ms Thymes. I neglected to tell you. I'm sorry." Mr. Dunn explained.

"Oh, okay, I'll just wait downstairs for the next forty five minutes." Ms Thymes said.

"No. That won't be necessary. Would you bring me a cup of coffee to the law library, please?" Mr. Dunn asked of Tabora.

The other partners each looked suspiciously at the other, some with smirks on their faces. Then they all proceeded in their own directions. Mr. Dunn's activities with some of the ladies around the office had long since been duly noted by his colleagues. So leaving him and Tabora to themselves was the very lease they all could do. Mr. Jasper passed by and stared in a disapproving manner at Mr. Dunn.

In the law library, Tabora closed the door and slowly leaned her back against it. She stared toward Mr. Dunn then smiled openly with the cup of piping hot coffee in her hand. Mr. Dunn, who sat at the far end of the long, wood table, looked up slowly as she walked toward him. He came to his feet, smoothed his tie in front of him, then released the only button holding his jacket closed. Tabora placed the coffee in front of him. Their eyes met. Playfully, her mouth opened and her tongue slowly rounded her lips.

His eyes were like ice, then widened at the sight of her display. They rushed madly into each other arms.

"I miss you so much," Tabora said.

He shushed her as he always did. While grinning with both hands on her shoulders he broke her from their steamy embrace.

"I know you miss this, Tabora." He said, then he assisted her downward to where he wanted her. He loved the way she gave him head, but not as much as he loved having her raised, brown legs straddled over his lily white shoulders while he licked the walls of her pussy until she exploded. He didn't realize just how much he really cared for Tabora until he saw actual footage of her in bed with another man; she seemed to enjoy the intense love making that took place on each of the encounters she partook in. Though he'd put her up to making out with the unsuspecting sucker, it crushed his heart to see her so caught up in the sweaty episodes she endured.

Hours later, in his office down the hall, Omar stood with his right arm above his head and against the huge window pane behind his large, mahogany wood desk. His left hand juggled loose change in his left front pocket, while his forehead laid against his right arm. He stared out at the blanketing traffic below from his fourth floor office overlooking downtown Northwest Washington, D.C.

Thoughts of this afternoon's meeting with Tabora raced through his mind. They caused warm feelings throughout his body, and he let go of the loose change in his pocket and fondled himself. His reflection in the window pane revealed the glow on his face. Suddenly Janet popped into his mind, and his hard dick faltered from the thought. "Damn,

Janet is starting to suspect something is going on," he murmured. He thought it best to cancel his and Tabora's planned mid day meeting at the Renaissance Hotel, which had become her favorite downtown hotel as of late. He thought of how that freak always gets the same room like she's some sort of big shot, but he didn't care, as long as she paid for it.

Still, if he kept this afternoon's date with her, he thought that it would take everything he had left in him to satisfy her horny ass, and he would have no desire to make love to Janet tonight as he had promised her he would. He knew that Tabora would drain him sexually, leaving nothing for Janet, she always did.

He smiled and stroked his own ego when he thought of how Tabora all but threw herself on him about two months ago after he had broke it off with her just before he married Janet. "That girl missed this big rock," he muttered. Then thought, why else would she come back begging for it – Omar flinched.

Someone had just tapped lightly on his closed office door. *It's no one but Connie.* Before he turned to have Connie enter, the door opened quickly, then closed.

"Oh, it's you. Come in, Ms Thymes. What can I do for you?" Asked Omar. He waited until she got closer to him.

"You know you shouldn't be in here like this. What's wrong with you?" He gritted his teeth angrily. His head swivelled quickly toward the door then back to Tabora.

"Your secretary wasn't at her desk, so I thought I'd come in and see how you were doing. You know, with all that built up tension over who's gonna be assigned the big Tanners case, and all. I though"–

Before he knew it, he'd grabbed her. He didn't mind stroking that ass of hers, but it pissed him off for her to think that there was any kind of feeling involve in their relationship; she was just a piece of ass to him, and he needed her to get that through that thick drupe that she used for brains. Still he knew that he had to be careful, and keep it professional around the office.

"I'm fine Ms Thymes. Now if you'll excuse me . . . I thought I told you not to bother me on the job, huh."

Omar felt like slapping her face, but good, and his hand was poised to do so. She was trying his last nerve, but he could tell that she knew he wouldn't put his foot up her ass on the job.

Tabora looked back toward the closed office door, and then walked toward Omar. She appeared totally defiant, and set on having her way with him.

Is this whore crazy, he thought? He pushed her away, forcefully.

"Let's stop with all the formalities, Omar . . . I can tell you who is going to be assigned that big case, that is, if you'll be nice to me." Once she was near to him, she fondled Omar briefly.

His left hand squeezed the back of the leather chair as the stroke of her hand sent trimmers through his body. He fought the temptation to give in to her, but did he ever want her to continue?

Tabora on the other hand, was as confident as ever as she groped him more. She had come a long way since the days of being a little horny, inexperience girl. These days she knew exactly what she wanted from a man, and exactly how to prep him to deliver the goods.

"Ooh, hh, I'll take that as a firm yes." She said after feeling Omar's rise, then she started to go down on him where he stood behind the chair.

Omar finally pushed her away again.

"I told you before, Tabora, if you couldn't steer clear of me at work, the affair would end, and this is it, it's over. Now get the fuck out of here before I forget where I am and numb that pretty Lil face of yours."

Tabora's eyes widened, and she seemed disgusted, she attempted to step toward him again, this time, forcefully, and determination was displayed throughout her face.

He grabbed her firmly by her left arm, and yanked her closer to him. "I want you out of here," he said. He led her around his desk then pushed her away again.

No sooner than Omar ordered Tabora out, the door to his office swung open.

"I'm sorry Mr. Johnson." His secretary, Connie said.

"Don't be, Connie, Ms Thymes was just leaving. Weren't you?"

"Mr. Johnson." Connie said, then nodded her head toward the opened door. "Mr. Dunn is here to see you."

Immediately upon hearing Mr. Dunn's name, Tabora adjusted her blouse and patted the sides of her hair. When in control of her composer, Tabora strutted out. She glanced under eyed at Mr. Dunn then rushed away.

Mr. Dunn, in turn, rushed into Omar's office. He looked around. Frantically he searched for some sign of what may have taken place. He finally looked at Omar.

"What went on in here, Mr. Johnson? And why is Ms Thymes upset?"

"Hey, Mr. Dunn, it's not what it looks like. I asked her to leave"–

"I guess I was right in my assessment of you," said Mr. Dunn, before Connie interrupted.

"Mr. Dunn, it's true. I heard Mr. Johnson when he asked Ms Thymes to leave."

"You stay out of this Connie if you know what's good for you. And you, Mr. Johnson, you may as well know now, you will not be assigned the Tanner's case."

Mr. Dunn leveled a stern stare in Connie's direction, then turned and stormed out of the office.

"Mr. Dunn, wait, what do you mean? Wait, dam'it, I can explain." Omar finally shouted.

"Save it, Mr. Johnson, you're skating on thin ice as it is," Mr. Dunn said, then hurried away.

"I'm really sorry, Mr. Johnson, I didn't know she was in here." Connie said, with both tightly closed fists clinched beneath her chin.

"It's okay, Connie, really. None of this is your fault."

Omar rounded his desk and fell hard into its leather cushioned seat bottom. He became emotional as he stared at Janet's photograph on the left side corner of his desk. "Man, if this shit gets out," he murmured, "Connie," he said, "I'd like to be alone for a few minutes, if you will."

"Oh, yes. I'll hold all of your calls."

Momentarily stunned by the depressing events, Omar watched quietly as Connie closed the door behind her.

It had taken every muscle in his body, and every form of reasoning he could muster to keep Omar calm. He wanted to break something, or, perhaps, someone. He unconsciously rubbed the palms of his hands together until they were hot. He leaned back in his chair. Did Mr. Dunn mean that I was not chosen to handle the Tanner case, or did he mean that I would not be selected because of what he suspects went on with Ms, Thymes and him?

As an astute attorney would, Omar thought it best to dissect each of Mr. Dunn's words, and tried to make sense of what he may have meant. But amidst all the confusion that took place, he realized he didn't exactly know what Mr. Dunn actually said. He sprang forward, pressed the intercom button: "Connie, would you get Mr. Dunn on the line for me, please."

"Yes, Mr. Johnson."

Moments later Connie buzzed Omar back.

"Mr. Johnson, Mr. Dunn has left for a meeting and will be out the remainder of the day. Connie rested her forehead in the palm of her right hand and let out a sigh. "Lord, what has that girl got Mr. Johnson into?" she muttered, then heard the door behind her open.

Mr. Johnson stormed out of his office and passed Connie's desk.

"Cancel my day please Connie."

"Sure will, Mr. Johnson, and I'll see you tomorrow." She shouted toward his fleeing image.

Still moving at a fast pace, Omar acknowledged Connie by raising his right hand behind him and shaking his briefcase toward her desk while still facing, and walking forward. He rushed down the hall to Mr. Jasper's office. If anyone could help him make sense of this whole situation, Mr. Jasper could; they had worked several cases together, and each considered the other a friend. It was Mr. Jasper who told Omar that he would push for him to be assigned the new case, but Mr. Dunn convinced the other members to give the huge case to someone else.

Mr. Jasper's secretary explained to Omar that he would be leaving tomorrow morning for a four-week trip to Connecticut to work with an important client, and by no means wanted to be disturbed.

A likely story, Omar thought. Except he remembered meeting and working with a client in Connecticut, through Mr. Jasper. It was their only Connecticut client. He remembers because the guy was a drug lord. Omar thought that the firm had ridded it self of that account long ago. But that was neither here nor there, Omar reasoned. He wanted answers concerning his future at the firm. This case was to be his big break, if they screw him around with the Tanner case, he may as well walk, find a firm where he would be better appreciated. Nonetheless, he felt that there was no need being hasty. He wanted to leave no stone unturned before that kind of talk set in.

"Are you certain there is no chance of him seeing me, Mrs. Brice?"

"As a matter of fact, I am." She replied, more direct than snobbish.

It didn't matter, though, Omar had other troubles that were more pressing and important then Mrs. Brice's sharp tongue; he decided to leave the building.

In the lobby, on his way to the elevator, Omar stared silently toward Tabora, who turned her head in the other direction upon seeing him. Omar paused, he wished he had her in that hotel room right now; he would certainly lay hands on her ass. He knew that he had to leave immediately to avoid doing something he'd regret later, so he turned and stormed out of the lobby. "Ops," he said, then he looked up.

"Excuse me, sir," Omar said, when he bumped the huge man who entered into the office lobby as he exited.

"It's cool, my man," the big guy replied, then turned his attention to Tabora.

"How are you doing today, sweetheart?" asked the big guy, he wiped the shine of sweat from his shiny brow.

"I'm fine, Mr. Kelly," Tabora responded, her legs swung out and in beneath her desk. She thought of how it would feel to be held in his strong arms, momentarily.

"Is he in?" Big Kelly asked.

"Huh, oh yes, he should be waiting for you as usual."

In the back office Big Kelly sat and listened to Mr. Jasper as he explained the latest details about the men suspected of robbing the drop house that night. As it turned out, Millhouse, Doo-Dirty, and Big Ed had suddenly begun making a name for themselves in the dope business, and didn't seem to care that the drugs were stolen. It didn't take Mr. J's eyes and ears on the streets long at all to figure out who had embarrassed him. He had become the laughing stock of Washington's downtown, white collar drug handlers, but now it was his turn for redemption, a time to get his good name back.

"It's like I told you," Mr. Jasper said, "the tri–state area would not be big enough for punks like those guys to hide. They may not have known it, but they stole from me, and I won't tolerate the shit."

"Actually, Mr. J, it was your product, but they stole from me too, and they made me look bad." Big Kelly admitted, cautiously.

This big ape is lucky to still be alive, Mr. J. thought, staring silently at him, and it didn't matter that his money was stolen that night, he didn't follow my instructions. Mr. J. was not one to forget the details, and Big Kelly owed him dearly for sparing his life after the robbery took place.

"Well, had you followed my instructions that night I don't believe any of this shit would have happened, so let's not piss me off about it, okay? I called you in here because I finally know the whereabouts of the robbers. Here, take this phone number. It's the number to my men out following the two of them right now. I understand there are three of the little cock roaches, if you're lucky they'll lead you to the other one. But I want you to make an example of those two. Ah, by the way, your big ass is still living because of our years together, but if you fuck this up I'll forget I ever met you."

"Don't you worry yourself over that," Big Kelly said, "I've got people ready to move in on their ass right now as we speak? Is that it?"

"That's it."

Mr. J. fanned him away with a right backhand motion then he turned his chair toward the large window behind him.

6

Baby Chris had just left the office of his investment counselor, Janet Johnson, earlier that afternoon, and was feeling proud of himself in fact, for wisely leaving the hustle game behind. While driving, he thought how too many hustlers stayed around the game too long, many of them because they knew of no other way except the hustle. Consequently they got busted, and others die at the hands of a jealous foe, or the law. Either way, he thought, they lose it all.

Chris felt that he was different now. He wanted more out of life and he learned with ambitious intent ways of improving his life. He'd come to understand the benefits of utilizing legitimate business practices to grow his money. And since he'd amassed a large sum of money from the hustle, he felt that it was only fitting that he elevated himself to the level of the hustle game, which was to systematically work his way to becoming a rich capitalist.

Still, old habits die hard, and Baby Chris hadn't completely broken the habit of hanging out and reminiscing old bullshit with his old friends at some of their old stomping grounds. His thinking was that of an optimist, and if the fellas liked what the white collar hustle produced for him, maybe they would be inclined to give up the street hustle and join his new and safe way of doing business.

He ended up selling his portion of the dope from the robbery to Millhouse, Doo-Dirty, and Ed, he didn't want to take the chance of 'going down' on a drug charge, particularly since he had his cash earning legal dividends now. Though he didn't see them all the time anymore, he often thought about the fellas.

He'd just parked in front of his house when he heard a car horn blow from across the street. He turned slowly then did a double-take. Speak of the devil!

"What up, boy?" he shouted across the street. It was Millhouse and Ed, but Doo-Dirty was no where insight.

"What are you up to Chris?" Millhouse asked, as he pushed his glasses up on his nose. "Come and take a ride with us, fool."

Baby Chris thought about it for a moment. He knew he'd promised Janet that the two of them would meet in exactly two hours, and he knew straight-up that he didn't want to miss what she had in store for him, but what the hell, he thought, he should be back by then. He gestured with his raised hand for Millhouse and Big Ed to give him a minute; he went inside, but only for a moment. Upon his return he got into the car with his partners and they drove off. Neither of them noticed the caprice with the tinted windows parked a half block back, and on the other side of the street, when they drove off.

The three friends sat in the sunny parking lot of the Armstrong Apartment Complex, laughing, drinking beer and smoking blunts. The car's stereo rattled the entire body of the chevy impala, still, Big Ed was seated in the front seat on the passenger's side, bobbing his head to the sounds of the Dirty South; Baby, Lil Wayne, and marinating in the smoke-filled compartment. Millhouse and Baby Chris leaned against the front fender of the impala.

"So how long has Doo-Dirty's crazy ass been locked down?" Baby Chris asked.

It turned out Doo-Dirty had been picked up on some charge that had nothing to do with robbery or murder, and had eight more months of lock down left.

"He's been gone about a month, and I don't have to tell you how much I miss his ass already, huh?" Millhouse replied.

"Yeah, I know, yo. Hey man, whatever happen to your girl, au, Tabora?"

"Shit, since me and my girl split, Tabora comes over a couple times every couple of months or so, but she is supposed to be in love with some married lawyer. Ha, that girl is an animal in bed, yo," Millhouse said, then he changed the conversation.

"So how is living the good clean life been treating you, brah? You' looking good, that's for sure."

"It's all good, man," said Chris, "and it's like I said, I'm no angle or no shit like that, man I just didn't like taking all those chances of being caught or killed, you know. I wanted to have something to show for my troubles that's all. And right now shit is looking good."

"That's good, brah, I'm happy for you," said Millhouse, "Maybe one day I'll be able to see that far ahead in my life, you know? You should be happy that you were able to move on, being stuck here is getting old real fast, man."

"Yeah, I hear you. You know, it should be mandatory that all street hustlers take their earnings and move up to the white collar hustle and then start living the way the rest of these motha fuckas live, you know?"

"With brothers like you showing us the way, I believe it'll happen for us all one day." Millhouse said. He pushed up on his glasses and stared toward the end of the parking lot. "What are those niggas doing cruising the parking lot?"

Millhouse's glassy eyes squinted as he stare in an attempt to see who was inside of the slow cruising car coming toward them.

"I can't tell who the fuck that is, man." Baby Chris said, that looks –

Ed jumped up from the passenger seat and yelled over the music. "Might be trouble, 'G', that's Big Kelly's rollers."

"Damn sure is," Millhouse murmured, then he turned to Baby Chris.

"You don't need to be here, Chris, go on, take a walk, my nigga."

"Walk? Where the fuck to?"

Big Ed pulled his pistol and held it low and out of sight.

Millhouse placed his along the side of his right leg. They all waited.

"Chris, get the fuck on the other side of the car, man, these niggas might start blazing."

"Yeah, no shit" –

Baby Chris, who was unarmed, moved to reposition himself on the other side of the car when the low rider that the strangers drove up in, sprang up high above the ground; it was apparently fitted with air shocks and bounced once. Squealing from the car's front tires ensued and the right side windows came down. Within a few seconds bodies and weapons appeared. Ed and Millhouse fired their pistols first and scattered for cover. Baby Chris hadn't reached a safe place yet, and scurried to find cover. However, it seemed one of the shooters had placed him in his sight, and Baby Chris was the first to go down as he attempted to round the front of the impala.

"Ugh, fuck, I been shot, oh, hh, shit." He cried out for help, but too much was happening too fast. No one knew that Baby Chris was shot.

Millhouse ducked behind a parked van when the semiautomatic weapons from the intruders' car riddled the van, forcing Millhouse to make a move for better cover. The sound of gun fire and piercing metal was all around. Pop . . . pop . . . pop.

He finally looked over and saw Baby Chris beside the impala, motionless.

Then he watched as Ed attempted to run across to the other side of the parking lot. He fired round after round, but it was all in vain. His clip emptied and —

Big Kelly's men sprang out of the left side window and mowed Ed down. "Ugh, shit," he screamed. Ed's body jerked backwards before he slid face first and toppled over, his body came to rest under the rear of a parked car.

Millhouse attempted to run for cover behind an apartment building when he was darted with bullets. He fell to the ground, rolled over, as if in pain, then lied still. One of Kelly's men got out of the car and started toward Millhouse, who lay still on his back until Big Kelly's man was close enough. . . Pop . . . pop. Millhouse took him down and got up to run when he screamed in pain, "Ugh, shit." He fell into the grass face first. The car sped off.

* * *

Tabora took a serious chance and called Omar's secretary, Connie, moments after he stormed out of the lobby. After a couple of months of the harsh physical and mental abuse from both men on her job, Tabora needed someone to talk to, and the two women talked for better than an hour. Connie listened, and was beside herself.

"He deals drugs too? Mr. Dunn and Mr. Jasper? Girl, why does he tell you all these things?"

"He loves me," Tabora explained, "We've been seeing each other for almost three years or so."

"Girl, I think everyone felt something was going on between you two, but how can you say he loves you? You just told me he beats you. He threatens you. Why don't you leave that relationship alone?"

"He said if I tried to leave him he would have me" –

"Have you what, girl," Connie asked?

"Have me killed," Tabora replied.

"Killed? Shit, girl, it sounds like you are in over your head, you should go to the police."

"I can't."

Connie could hear the fear in Tabora's voice and felt bad for her. However, an hour ago Connie would not have helped Tabora out of quicksand if her life depended on it, she thought. Not after the way Tabora had upset her boss, Omar. But when Connie heard what Tabora had been going through in her office affairs, it made her have some degree of compassion for her. And Mr. Dunn, she'd heard some things around the office about him, but had no idea he was such an ass. Connie broke the silence.

"Well, girlfriend, I don't know what else to suggest."

"Look. I'm okay. I wanted to talk to you so you could tell Omar, then maybe he won't be so angry with me later on when other information start getting out."

"You mean to tell be that there's more to this than what you've told me?"

"Yes, but I can't talk about it, okay?"

"Okay then. I don't know what you thought you were doing this morning in Mr. Johnson's office, but he wasn't very happy when he left."

* * *

That evening before going home to an empty house, Marc Dunn drove to Maryland and stopped in on Tabora. The two of them sat in her bed room talking until he suggested that she go into the bath room and slip into something special for him. She had just gone in when he removed the manilla envelope from beneath his suit coat. The envelope contained a book listing all the information about Mr. Jasper's along with others at the law firm, involvement in the drug trade. He'd also placed most of the cash he'd made while pretending he was in with Mr. J., in a locker at the gym where he works out; the key, and location to the locker was inside the book also.

He could never let his wife know that he had any involvement in the drug business, even if it was only to try and find out exactly how his father was killed. He trusted Tabora, and wanted her to have the money and information. If something was to happen to him, he knew that she would know what to do.

He roamed her room wondering where he should place the package when he thought he heard her about to come out. He quickly opened the door to a night stand located next to her bed, and he stuffed the package inside. He then turned and immediately left the bedroom, then looked around once before exiting her apartment.

7

That night at their modest estate in Mount Vernon, Virginia, where Omar was usually comfortable and felt well secluded from the outside rigors of Washington's downtown metropolis, he was everything but. He told Janet about the encounter with Tabora and hoped she would understand that nothing happened between them. His explanation of what happened, though true as it may have been, sounded some what suspect, particularly in light of his and Tabora's passed relationship, which Janet had been made aware of in the beginning. Janet had been pouting for the better part of the evening, but it wasn't because of Omar's infidelities, it was because of Baby Chris's death earlier that day.

It hurt her so bad to find out on the news that he was killed. She'd worked with him professionally for months without a hitch, but as soon as she decided to go all the way and get intimate with him, he goes and gets himself killed. It seemed as though she was destined to be at the mercy of Omar's cheating ass when it came to being loved, and she hated the thought of it. Listen to him, she thought, she finally just wished he'd shut his slut smelling ass up for a change.

"C'mon, baby, talk to me, say something. It's not like I did something to provoke Tabora," Omar said.

Unfortunately, when Omar mentioned Tabora's name it fermented hostel feelings deep inside of Janet that she'd harbored for months. And tonight she was in just the mood to tell him a thing or two about himself and those 'scank' whores he'd been involved with.

"Now you see," Janet began. "You had to bring that whore Tabora's name up in our house again." Janet placed her left leg atop the bed as she climbed in and noticed Omar's eyes as they cruised toward her crotch. She laid her head on an elevated pillow to his left.

"I trusted you with her after you said that the two of you were finished Omar, and then something like that happens. What am I to think?"

"You don't have to think shit, I've told you more than once that there's nothing going on between Tabora and me." Omar sat up next to Janet and grabbed her left arm.

"You've been putting my sex needs off all this week, woman, and now you're using some bullshit about Tabora that never took place to further deprive me of having sex with you. I've given up all of that running around, and you still won't fuck me? You think I don't know the real reason your ass is feeling so bad. Is it because of that thug ass nigga Chris, your so-called client? If that boy hadn't been killed, I'd kick his young ass, cause I know you fucked him, bitch."

"Release my arm, Omar," Janet shouted then pulled away from his grip.

She thought how she certainly would have fucked Baby Chris had he lived long enough to meet her this afternoon as they had planned, but she didn't, so she ignored Omar's comment for the moment. She saw the lust in his eyes when he looked at her. He tried to disguise it with anger. She felt she had his lying ass right where she wanted him: he needed her loving for a change and she just wasn't having his roaming dick sliding in and out of her like she was one of his cheap whores.

Omar had never struck her before, though she had seen him angry in the past. That in itself led her to believe that he would never abuse her in any way. So she laid back on her pillow atop the covers with her long legs crossed sporting his favorite pink neglige; she knew exactly what to do to get a rise out of him sexually, but since he claimed he would have put a foot in Baby Chris' ass, knowing that Chris was no longer a factor, she thought she'd cross into bounders where she'd never ventured before with him. She looked at his sorry ass face, and with a cunning smirk on hers, she began.

"Why didn't you ever go to Mr. Dunn and confront him about not assigning you the Tanner case? The case is all over the television set, that's suppose to be your case. Tell me, why didn't you? See you can tell me about what you would do someone whose dead, but why didn't you confront Mr. Dunn. What's up with that?"

"What are you insinuating, woman," Omar asked? "Are you saying that I don't handle my business? Is that it?" Omar bolted upright in a fury and with startling swiftness he'd straddled Janet's body.

The agitating smile on Janet's face had turned to that of bewilderment, and just that fast she wondered just what the hell her mouth had gotten her into; she could see the burning rage in his eyes, and anger controlled every shiny black muscle in his body.

"I'm your husband, dam-it." He pulled and ripped the upper half of her neglige. His eyes glared as though he was seeing her firm, caramel breast for the first time.

"Yeah, now what do you think about that, huh?" He clasped both her hands with his and leaned down slowly and kissed her breast, her neck.

Janet squirmed about the bed beneath his firm wrestlers' pin-down. She knew Omar was not joking, and she had never seen him in such a rage before. Perhaps she had gone too far in her attempts to belittle him. She screamed. "Omar, I don't want to do this, please, get off of me."

Janet screamed louder when he ripped the lower half of her neglige while using his brute strength to hold her down.

"Stop playing, girl," Omar shouted, as he forced his muscular body between her legs of resistance. "You wouldn't have been teasing me if you didn't want it."

Omar struggled momentarily. She hit him with every once of strength left in her freed left hand, but to no avail. Her struggle was all for naught, and she felt his hard dick as it slid partially inside of her. She wiggled and wrestled beneath his mass, yet knowing she had no defense for his attack. Suddenly she stopped breathing. Her mouth was wide opened, momentarily, and every muscle in her body froze; she'd felt his large, rigid muscle when it slid deeper inside of her, filling every cavity of flesh, it seemed.

He whaled up and down like a mad man when she suddenly laid still and cried. His dark, sweaty body slid up and down against hers. His looming lips tried to capture hers, as she swung her head from left to right in total defiance.

He had been putting her off sexually for months, but as he forcibly humped up and down inside of her, he wondered why? Her warm pussy sent pleasure all the way to the tips of his toes, why, he wondered? He'd forgotten ecstasies she sent through his body, even without freaking him like Tabora did.

"Stop, you mother fucker," she screamed. His clammy body had never bothered her in the past during consenting sex, tonight, however, she hated everything about him.

Nonetheless, the more she twisted and turned in an effort to fight him off, the more she found herself fighting the strong desire to reciprocate, to satisfy her own needs.

He was about to come, and she could tell by his galloping strides. What's more important is the fact that she too was coming, and it pissed her off that she enjoyed the feeling after so many months. She found herself crying out in anger, while galloping stride for stride with him, churning out feelings, pelvises' bumping loudly against each other. Finally, they both cried out simultaneously; her body trembled when she came. She hated him so, but at that moment, she wanted more of him, but finally laid still in protest.

"Come on, woman," Omar managed, winded yet reeling with vigor. He continued. "That's why we don't have sex now, look at you, just laying there like a fucking log." Omar complained, yet he carried out his assault on Janet to the end. "Ha, ha, yeah, girl you need to stop all that fussing, I'm your husband, shit, what are you laying around crying about?"

When finished, he climbed off her and fell hard onto his pillow next to her.

Janet quietly reached over to the night stand next to the bed and grabbed the alarm clock –

"Ugh, shit," Omar shouted, "what's your damn problem, woman?"

He raised his right hand to his face then looked at the blood as it trickled down his fingers. Janet had thrown the alarm clock and struck Omar on the right side of his face and caused a small cut just below his eye brow.

"Bitch, I was just joking with you the first time, but now you've pissed me off.," Omar said. He leaned over and struck her on her face, causing her mouth to bleed. He grabbed her and pulled her to him. He wrestled her until he finally got her body over his knees, and he began spanking her naked ass as she screamed.

The phone rang and Omar stopped long enough to lean over and quickly see on the caller ID box that it was Connie from work, and without further hesitation, he ignored it and continued his business.

"You see if I was one of those thug-ass youngsters like your so-called client, Chris was, I'd be planting my foot in your ass for cutting my face with the clock, but you know I love you too much to do that. So take this ass whipping and shut the fuck up. And don't you ever question my manhood again, especially when it comes to those punk ass white boys at that law office. I'm your man."

He spanked her harder then leaned down and kissed her bruised butt cheeks.

"Girl you don't know nothing about that kinda love making, do you?"

Omar lifted her up and threw her against the pillow where she grabbed the spread from the bed to cover herself. She laid still and cried.

* * *

Omar exited the elevator and walked briskly through the double doors leading to the lobby and Tabora's work station. His and Tabora's eyes met, but briefly.

"Good morning, Ms Thymes."

"Mr. Johnson." She replied, then continued her morning routine. Omar proceeded along the hallway to the right of Tabora's desk. He passed Connie at the coffee station.

"Morning, Connie," he said, in a low whisper. He slowed his pace and whispered again to her. "Meet me in my office, please."

"Sure, right away, Mr. Johnson," Connie replied. She smiled at the co-worker next to her then proceeded to rush with the preparation of her coffee, and followed close behind Omar.

"You okay this morning, Connie?"

"I'm fine . . . Listen, Mr. Johnson, I didn't mean to interfere in your business."

"No, no, come on in and sit down. You know. I must have fallen asleep early last night. I didn't get your message until this morning, and I'm dying to hear more."

"Oh that. I figured you might be interested in knowing about that right away, and that's why I left the message on your phone. Oh, and Ms Thymes wanted me to apologize to you for her conduct yesterday."

"Yeah, okay, but get back to the part about how they selected Scott for the big Tanner case." Omar replied. Omar understood from Connie's message that Mr. Dunn was up to his ears in drug trafficking. That was all good, but he wanted to be briefed on the office matters that had all but stopped his progression at the law firm; his mind was focused on learning who was responsible for him not getting the Tanner's case.

"Ms Thymes had mentioned that Mr. Jasper and the others had selected you when Mr. Dunn stood up and gave this long speech about why he thought Scott was best for the case, then he all but threatened the others until the selection went his way, against Mr. Jasper's wishes."

Omar could not believe it. It explained everything, and it may also be the reason he was passed over twice for major cases during prior selections. The bad vibes he had been feeling where Mr. Dunn was concerned were not just fragments of his imagination. Everything he felt was all real. The fact that Tabora was sleeping with Mr. Dunn may explain why it appeared he had it out for Omar all along. Omar wondered silently how would Mr. Dunn react if he knew that his girl Tabora had come running back to him, and had been sleeping with him for the past couple of months? He could hardly contain the smile on his face.

"There is one other thing, though," Connie said, breaking the silence. "I took the liberty of asking, Joyce, Mr. Dunn's secretary, to fit you into his schedule, and she got you in for eleven o: clock today. I hope it's okay that I did that."

"That's good, Connie." Mr. Johnson said, slowly shaking his head up and down. "As a matter of fact, that's very good, Connie. By then I'll have plenty to say to that snake. Thanks Connie."

Omar watched as Connie walked out and closed the door behind her. He leaned back in his chair. "I wish that punk Marc Dunn would try and handle me the way he handles Tabora's ass, I just need him to give me one excuse to take him down," he muttered then looked at his watch and smiled; it wouldn't be long before he would be face to face with the one man who apparently had been responsible for many of Omar's career set backs.

8

Mr. Dunn sat back comfortably in the brown leather chair. His elbows rested on each of the padded arms rests. He rolled the yellow number two pencil around between the fingers of both his hands, slightly below his eye level. The smirk on his face chiseled away at Omar's will to maintain the low level of tolerance he had left, as he sat across the desk from Mr. Dunn.

"You can sit there like you don't give a shit, but I'm telling you I know about the drug ring as well as your threatening Ms Thymes. I also know about how you manipulated the others to prevent me from handling cases that you knew I was most qualified to handle.

"So, what do you intend to do with that information, Omar?"

"Oh, I don't know, Marc." Omar said. " I could sue the firm and then, maybe, expose your involvement in the distribution of drugs, or vice versa. Which do you prefer I do first, Marc?"

Mr. Dunn smiled and maintained his calm demeanor before he said. "Mr. Johnson, you do not want to engage me in this way. You won't win, and I can assure you of that."

All of Marc's thoughts were of the womanizer who sat in front of him pretending to be a man; Tabora had told him of the beatings she'd taken from Omar when he got angry with her, for that reason alone

Marc would love to teach the sissy a lesson in manhood. He wished the punk would give him a reason to bounce him around his office a little. His face reeked of discontent, as he stared across the desk at Omar.

"Really. Then what will you say if I told you I have a witness who'll testify against you on the drug counts?" Omar countered, then he confidently eased back in his chair. He felt he had wounded his adversary when he saw the look on Mr. Dunn's face turn sour. But it wasn't enough, Omar wanted to see the sucker fall harder. This was the man that his wife Janet implied that he was afraid of. Omar would love nothing better than to relinquish the thought from her mind completely, and today was as good a day as any to put it to rest. He also felt like kicking his ass for the beatings Tabora said he'd given her. There was no chance of the white boy reporting him if he was to kick a mud hole in his ass behind the closed doors of his office, simply because of the drug information that he holds over Marc's head.

However, Marc, who was still calmly seated behind his desk, slowly lowered the yellow pencil. He placed it atop the desk in front of him. He removed a television remote control device from the right side top drawer, just in front of a loaded pistol that he kept, then finally broke his silence.

"Tell me something, Mr. Johnson. How do you think Janet would feel if she found out about you and Ms Thymes's little love connections?"

"Please. That's old news Marc, babe. Ha. Janet knows about every detail. So . . . is that all you bring to the table?" Omar said as he rose to his feet. He leaned over the well-kept desk top and stated sternly.

"I may not have a job after this, but you'll be finished also, you son of a bitch." He turned and headed to the door. "I'll see you in court, motha fucker."

"Wait, Mr. Johnson, please," shouted Mr. Dunn. There seemed to be a sense of urgency in his voice that permeated the confines of the office.

Omar stopped dead in his tracks, and tried to contain the blush on his face. He could hear it in the coward's voice that this was the moment he had waited for. He had Mr. Dunn's young smart ass ready to kiss his ass if he thought it would save his own. He wondered what concession the defeated, no-good bastard was willing to part with, in order to save his ass. Omar turned slowly and looked confidently toward Mr. Dunn, and knew that Mr. Dunn could see the merciless expression frozen on his face.

"What is it, Marc? Getting a little too warm in here for you?"

Mr. Dunn merely grinned, however, and turned to the television screen that popped up from the back of the bar to his right. He turned back to face Omar, and all the time he watched Omar's face and saw how curiosity had draped him entirely; his eyes swept from the rising screen to Mr. Dunn, and back. Mr. Dunn proceeded and pushed the 'on' button on the remote control.

"Quite the contrary, Mr. Johnson. I think you would agree that the only friction causing it to warm up in here is right there on the television screen."

There they were. Omar and Tabora engaged in hot, steamy, 'doggy styled' sex. She moaned with passion and appeared to take great pleasure in the moment. His lower trunk pounded against her butt with great intensity. The meaty portion of her behind spread each time he slammed against that ass and settled deeper into her warm, wet flesh. Sweat poured from her body as she performed masterfully for the camera. And Omar could do nothing about it.

Like any good lawyer prior to a case, Omar probably would have like to have heard all of the information that Connie was suppose to relay to him earlier. It turned out that she neglected to tell him that Tabora had mentioned that there was more bad news to come, and that is why she was apologizing in advance.

"Oh, oh hh, I'm sorry Omar, but I can't hear you," Mr. Dunn said.

Omar couldn't believe it, he had to find out about the camera, and how he was made a fool of by both, Tabora and Mr. Dunn. It hurt him bad to hear that the camera had been placed inside the hotel room by Mr. Dunn himself, six weeks ago, when Tabora had agreed to renew her interest in him; it all came back to him, why she opted for the same room each time they rendezvoused.

Dunn grinned, at first, and then loud laughter ensued.

"You son of a – how did you get that camera into the room?" Omar asked, almost in tears. How could that happen, he thought.

"That wouldn't be your witness you're balling, would it, Omar, on this brand new, visibly dated disk, Mr. Johnson?" It seemed the tables had turned and Mr. Dunn was in the driver's seat. He didn't appear to want to stop to let Omar off, and continued to ride him.

Omar was finally tired of playing games, and stood near the door fuming. Still, he was mostly pissed because he knew that those pictures of him and Tabora were taken in the last two months, when he thought that Tabora had come running back to him because she couldn't do without his loving ways, his hanging testament. Now he realized that Mr. Dunn not only put Tabora up to it, but he took pictures of everything the two of them did together in the room.

Fuck it. This is it. Omar raced over to the bar in an attempt to retrieve the disk. He had seen enough, and was now ready to have his turns at the bat.

Mr. Dunn rose to his feet. He extended his left arm toward Omar's fast charging mass of anger.

"Don't come near my property Mr. Johnson," Mr. Dunn shouted loud enough to be heard in the outer hallway. Omar defiantly kept going toward the television set.

Mr. Dunn felt he had no other recourse. He suddenly swung his right hand and punched Omar hard to his stomach.

"Ugh, you bastard." Omar fell to his knees first, then he fell hard to the floor, grimacing in pain.

"Get up tough guy, before I kick you while you're down," Mr. Dunn said.

Omar seemed surprised by what he'd quickly reasoned to be a sneaky punch delivered by Mr. Dunn, but he wasn't having anymore of it. He snapped gingerly to his feet, and like the man that he was, he gave props.

"That was pretty good white boy, but now I'm gonna have to fuck you up."

He swung a sweet right cross at Mr. Dunn, who in turn skillfully side stepped the punch and made it appear as a wild delivery, before he gracefully punched Omar on the lower left side of his jaw. Omar stumbled before he fell limp against the bar, causing glasses to scatter and break. Mr. Dunn leaned over him.

"You get the hell out of my sight. You make me sick. And don't you even try to find work in this town you sorry sack of shit."

The office door swung open. Joyce, Mr. Dunn's secretary, screamed, and screamed again.

By then others had arrived. Mr. Dunn had man handled the womanizing bastard and now wanted him out of his office, and his life. He dragged Omar by the collar of his jacket and the waist of his pants to the door. The crowd moved backward to allow him room to maneuver. He threw Omar as far as he could into the general area of the office's hallway for all to see. Omar was battered and bleeding. He was just coming to his senses when he landed in the hallway and saw everyone looking on. He struggled to stand then walked stiltedly before falling against the wall of the hallway.

"I'll get you back, you bastard." Omar shouted, not totally lucid.

"Call security Joyce, have him escorted out of here for good."

"Yes sir, right away."

Connie, heard the loud voices from her desk, and pushed her way through the crowd of workers in time to see her battered boss struggle to stand on his feet. She ran up to him in an attempt to help him.

He jerked away from her then wiped blood from his face. He clumsily adjusted his suit coat and pants.

"Leave me alone woman. What's wrong with you? He shouted to Connie.

"But Mr"–

"But, my ass. I don't need you grabbing me like that. And what in hell are the rest of you looking at?"

Connie turned and walked away with tears in the wells of her eyes, and couldn't understand why she deserved that kind of treatment from Mr. Johnson.

Security personnel ran into the lobby of the law offices and questioned Tabora.

"Mr. Dunn. Where is Mr. Dunn's office? Come on ma'am, where is it?" one of them insisted.

"It's down the hall and to the right. What's this about?" Tabora asked.

The men turned and ran down the hall as directed, leaving Tabora closely behind chasing them. The security guards quickly apprehended Omar and began to forcibly removed him out of the law office, when Omar saw Tabora.

"You cheap whore. You're going to be sorry for what you did." he shouted as he passed Tabora. His words seemed muffled as the swelling around his jaw became more and more obvious.

Tabora's eye's widened. She wondered what she'd done so wrong that it made Omar so angry with her. She turned and peeked into the office of Mr. Dunn; he stood proudly behind his desk slapping the case with the disk of Tabora's and Omar sexual encounters against his left hand, while smiling deviously in her face.

Even Tabora figured instantly what the evil, conniving bastard must have done. She turned and walked angrily back toward her desk.

"Fucking men, always trying to gain the upper hand. Well I'm sick of all the bastards," she muttered. For some time now she'd been questioning all of her past relationships and found that none were worthy of the trouble that they brought to her. She felt that it was time she reverted back to satisfying herself the way she use to as a child, because men were so 'not what they seemed'.

Still, she wished it was a way she could make it up to Omar for the wrong she'd done to him. She thought of him as being her best friend Sara's cousin.

The guards finally cast Omar out of the building and onto the side walk. Embarrassed. He tugged on the lapels of his suit coat, dusted his pant leg, and stiltedly walked away.

9

"So Sara, how have you enjoyed your week so far?" asked Mr. James, Taylor's father. He tried as he had all week not to be so obvious when he stared at Sara's exquisite anatomy. Perhaps it was because he had been alone for so long that her every bodily move seemed to demand his undivided attention; Taylor's mother walked out on him three years ago, and since then he'd been bent on raising Taylor as best he could, sacrificing all else. But now, after a week of sharing his home with the likes of Sara, feelings inside of him that he thought died with the divorce were rekindled and highly active.

He found himself staring at Sara as she awkwardly repositioned herself on the sofa across from him. She turned him on in ways he hadn't allowed himself to be in all the years since his divorce, and he had no excuses for what he was feeling for the younger, attractive Sara.

The three of them sat in the living room to the right of the kitchen, laughing and talking over what began as a single drink to celebrate the culmination of the week long visit. No one knew that Sara, who seldom drank at all, would indulge as much as she had in the fifth of Scotch that sat in front of her almost emptied. Taylor seemed unhappy with Sara's unprecedented behavior. She would more than likely have some choice words for Sara on the trip back to school tomorrow morning;

Sara saw the look of disgust on Taylor's young freshmen face and felt the need to get her to loosen up.

She inadvertently opened her legs brazenly when she rose from the sofa, briefly exposing her panties. Mr. James sipped from his glass while he looked under eyed between her legs. Unaware, Sara stood and jubilantly walked to the other end of the sofa where Taylor sat, seemingly pouting. Sara stood over her and snapped her fingers to the soft music that filled the background and began to smile and shake her body. Her body swayed from left to right when she turned to Mr. James.

"I've had a great time Mr. James and I want to thank you for your hospitality, but do you see how your daughter is? She's no fun at all," Sara blurted out with a slur.

Sara had come to grips with her sexuality once she left her best friend Tabora back in Maryland and went off to college. After her freshman's year she not only found her sexuality, she also found that her women of choice were other young, wide-eyed freshmen women who'd just left their mother's nest; she'd learned that they were vulnerable, and easy to manipulate. She's since loved and broke the hearts of lots of freshmen's women; many of them did not understand that Sara was a butterfly, and not prone to commitment.

She was never after a relationship with anyone, only the opportunity to love and be utterly loved by any of a number of freshmen disciples she had amassed on campus. Still, she loved men, but relationships were few and many relationships between, not to mention how highly discrete they were. Her few encounters had never included dating men from her campus, and she wouldn't have had it any other way.

A senior now, and many relationships later, Sara found herself intrenched in an affair. And it was she who had strong feelings for her freshman's lover Taylor, but Taylor was proving to be a possessive little bitch, daddy's little girl. Sara agreed to this trip as a last attempt at salvaging what was left of their bumpy relationship, and until tonight, Sara thought that things were going really well. Not even Sara knew the full scope of how difficult it would be corralling Taylor's jealousy.

Sara turned and took another sip from her drink that sat on the coffee table and began dancing alone in the center of the living room floor.

Between Sara and her father, Taylor didn't seem to know who was more pathetic. She seemed angered as she had been during the entire week, whenever she saw the revealing look on her father's face when Sara entered into a room; he drooled like a hopeless fool, and Sara seemed to feed off of his scanning eyes. Taylor scowled as she stared across the room. He pretended to enjoy watching Sara dance when his shameless, lustful eyes said it all; he wanted to jump her bones with no regard for the fact that she's his daughter's best friend - best friends are what they made him believe they were, anyway.

Taylor wished now that Sara hadn't forced her, prior to their visit, to promise not to mention anything about their sexual relationship to her father; maybe her father would have some dignity about himself if he at least knew about the two of them; Taylor was bent on telling him all about her sexual preferences, and she felt like screaming it out loud to him now, but she didn't want to take the chance of losing Sara over it.

And speaking of Sara, as Taylor sat and watched her, she thought how she had never before seen her display any womanly mannerisms, but tonight, as she witnessed it, Sara was every bit of woman, gracefully swaying to the music's beat. She grinded and dipped her body, and with her left hand behind her neck, her right hand smoothed her right inner thigh repeatedly.

Taylor furrowed her brow. She stared with eyes of disdain, and caused crows feet to form around her eyes. Before Taylor knew what had happened, words of concern rushed angrily from her mouth.

"Sara. What are you doing? Why don't you sit down, or something?" Taylor blurted out.

"Awe, that's all right Taylor, go on and let Sara enjoy herself," Mr. James said, as he rose to his feet and joined Sara in the center of the floor. His heart raced out of control; would the younger, energetic woman be receptive to him, or pull away, embarrassing him in front of his daughter? It meant more to him to rise to his feet and find out than remaining seated fearing the results.

Sara smiled gleefully when she saw him approaching her, and spoke with a slur.

"Yeah, let's get this party started," she shouted. She immediately turned her back to Mr. James and placed both her hands on her knees. Mr. James placed both his hands shoulder high snapping his fingers and swerving his trunk. Sara smiled cheerfully as she pumped her young ass in and out, and backed up until she was firmly pressed against his crotch. Mr. James quickly dropped both hands and grabbed her around the waist. He shamelessly pulled and locked her raised butt against his hard dick and began to grind on her.

He dry-fucked her in the center of the living room floor. When he looked up to see his daughter's eyes of fire, searching him for any shame he might have had, he pretended to take the moment lightly.

"Oh Lord, you're gonna give the old man a heart attack," he shouted jokingly, yet he never stopped his all out 'pumping and grinding' ritual he had unleashed on Sara. He wished it were up to him to stop humping on Sara's soft, tender behind, but it wasn't. Music filled the room, the Scotch seemed to control his brain, and it was telling him that he was deep in Sara's warm hatch. He closed his eyes.

Sara was delighted by the sensation of his hard dick between the rear of her legs; her short skirt had long since risen above the cheeks of her butt. She liked it when Mr. James positioned his left leg between both of hers and pulled her even closer; she rode his solid flesh up and down his leg. She looked over her right shoulder and saw the intention on the face of Mr. James, and his eyes were still closed, while his head bobbed slowly back and forward; he felt the heat between her legs as the sensation rose to his head.

Taylor rose to her feet angrily, and stared momentarily in disbelief before she stormed, unnoticed out of the living room, and up the stairs to hers and Sara's bedroom.

Sara felt his stone-like dick stretched along his left leg, and she masterfully slid her raised behind up and down against him. She smiled and knew that the father figure behind her was getting great pleasure from her, and she too was hot and wet, and wanting more of him. Suddenly the music stopped, they both continued grinding, momentarily, Mr. James, it seemed, was in the midst of a climax, and desperately sought to ride the feeling out; he pulled her even closer against him, and trembled out of control while doggedly humping her.

When he finished, his eyes opened to see Sara staring up at him over her right shoulder; he wondered if she felt him tremble the way he did when he exploded for the first time in months.

They each smiled awkwardly at the other as Sara turned to face him. She slid her right hand through her short hair, sweaty, and licking her teasing lips, she threw her head slightly to the right.

He glanced toward the living room door cowardly for any sign of Taylor, and hoped to God that his little girl had left the room. As soon as he realized she had left and the two of them were alone, he abruptly placed both his hands on Sara's shoulders and pulled her closer to him.

They kissed passionately for a moment. Mr. James was seventeen years older then his daughter's older friend, but the moment seemed so right; he wanted that young, hot pussy, and he wanted it tonight, before she left in the morning.

"Come to my room, and let's have a drink there. Please. I need you so bad," Mr. James said.

"I can't. Taylor and I are. . . ."

"What? Best friends? I know that."

"Well we're best friends and you're her father. That wouldn't be right, now would it?"

"She's a big girl and we're two consenting adults, and tonight I want to love you like I know you've never been loved before," Mr. James whispered.

Sara's body twitched at the sound of those words. If there was one thing she'd learned during her off campus rendezvous with older men: they loved eating a younger girl's pussy as a means of getting her in bed; she also knew that his ultimate goal would be to try and get his dick wet.

As she stared into his lustful eyes, she saw the desperation, the uncertainty, and yet she thought of how right now, this minute, she would fuck him. But he seemed too passive, no charm. He appeared as just a frail old horny man, filled with desires. All she visioned was having him lapping her so good that it would cause a rooster's tail higher than a boat motor between her legs, and she couldn't wait.

"Let me go and check on Taylor and the two of us can go to your room and finish our discussion there, okay?"

"Okay, sure sweetheart, just hurry back."

Sara immediately turned to the coffee table and grabbed her drink. She consumed the remanding drink in one swallow. After placing the glass on the table, she precariously leaned closer to Mr. James and rounded his lips with her tongue. In a heated moment of passion he went to grab her. She pulled away and stood stiltedly in front of him for a moment. She laughed openly at her clumsy behavior before she placed her index finger to her puckered lips.

"Shush!" She sounded, then turned and staggered while exiting the living room. She approached and walked up the stairs gingerly to the room she and Taylor shared. There was something taking place inside of Sara, and she was certain that liquor was not the stimulus that made her want to hurry back down stairs and into the arms of Mr. James; she had conflicting urges, and a need to see them through.

She opened the door to the dimly lit bedroom and slowly entered. Taylor laid atop the covers in a sprawling position dressed in only her panties. Sara stood over the bed staring down at her breast. She leaned down and softly kissed Taylor's neck, then her breast. Sara placed her right hand between Taylor's thighs and slowly massaged her pussy while she kissed her navel, her thighs.

"Oh hh, ugh." Taylor moaned as both her knees rose half way upward and her pelvis churned slowly.

On a sober night a mere touch of Sara's hand against her young mate's pussy would have aroused her completely out of her sleep prepared to roll around the sheets with Sara for as long as her juices lasted. But tonight she too had a lot to drink, and had apparently cried herself into a deep sleep.

Sara jerked her right hand out from between Taylor's legs and smiled solemnly when she was certain that Taylor was asleep.

"Get your rest babe, I'll be back for your fresh ass later," Sara muttered. She rose and stepped back, away from the bed, and left the room.

Sara lay in the center of Mr. James' bed with both her legs raised above his shoulders. Her eyes were closed. Both his hands extended upward cupping both her hard nipples. Her body churned hard and furiously. His hot, firm tongue darted in and out of her pussy with precision. She could care less if she never saw his pathetic face again, at this point, as long as it remained between her legs.

Suddenly she locked both her feet around his neck and her heels rested along his back. With both her hands flat against the bed, she forced her trunk hard against his face, and he defiantly held firm his position in almost suffocating fashion while her body pushed, begging for more. She grinded, twisted and turned when he caused her to come.

"Oh, hh, shit. You motha fucka, you," she moaned. Her legs fell hard to the bed on either side of him.

While she drifted aloft with pleasure throughout her body, he eased his body up in preparation to mount her proper, except Sara wasn't feeling womanly anymore. And the old man made her sick to her stomach.

Mr. James had no way of knowing that Sara would not reciprocate, and that she would refuse him the pleasure of wetting his dick, something he badly desired.

"Stop now, go head on, you old fool," she said, pushing him away and off of her.

"What, bitch?" He slapped her hard on her face. Anger, like air, filled the bedroom it seemed.

Everywhere she turned to escape his burning desires, he was all over her. He forced her firmly against the mattress with his elbow pressed hard against her neck; she wanted to scream but couldn't.

He forced his way on her and finally felt her warm, wet kitty against his rod. He long stroked her at first, but within seconds, it seemed, his strokes were short and vicious. He pounded against her then sank deep down to the bone before his sweaty body fell against hers. Though it only took seconds to achieve, Mr. James seemed to savior the moment. "Whew, shit," he said, still slowly churning inside of her; he trembled intermittently.

Sara attempted to push his drunk ass off of her with all the strength she had left in her body. Then she looked over his shoulders, in the doorway. It was Taylor, and she charged the bed with a large butcher's knife in her hand. Sara pushed but could not remove his mass of dead weight from atop her. Suddenly she heard the loudest scream she'd ever heard in her life, and it was directly in her ear. But in an instant, Sara screamed also when Mr. James rammed his hard rock deeper inside of her upon feeling the knife's blade in his back.

Taylor had driven the knife deep into her father's back, and continued to stab him while she screamed also.

"You son of a bitch, why, why," is all she repeated as his screams finally subsided.

He was still inside of Sara, but barely, when the two of them pushed him off of her, and Sara immediately feared for her life.

"Girl, your father raped me, I swear it," she pleaded.

"Sara you get your things and get your fucking ass out of my house, and out of my life, you no-good bitch."

"Babe, look, I wasn't trying to hurt you" –

"Now, you tramp, now!" Taylor wielded the knife recklessly, and Sara realized that the safest thing at that time was to obey, and she did.

* * *

"Look babe I said that I was sorry about the other night so why don't you move on back home?" Omar asked Janet.

Janet just stood staring at Omar's face, because she'd left him on the night he raped her, she hadn't had a chance to see him. She turned away from him when she could no longer hold in the laughter.

"What? What the fuck are you laughing at, bitch?"

"I'm laughing at your ass, and I'm not afraid of you anymore," she replied. "Look at you. Your face is all swollen. You sound as if there's shit in your mouth when you speak, and all you can say is that you had a run in with Dunn at work. It's obvious that something ran into your ass, but all week you seemed to not want to talk about what exactly happened, over the phone, and the only reason I came this evening was to find out what happened."

"Look, I'm trying to be civil with your ass and all you seem to want to do is start a fight." Omar shouted across the bedroom.

"Civil. Omar you raped me the other night, now, you want to be civil. I don't think so Mr. . . . I'm so tough when it comes to women, but look at my sorry ass now. You say you need me to stay here with you. Then I'll ask you again. What happened the other day at the office? Can you be civil enough to explain that?"

Janet cared less how she made Omar feel and he could sense the hatred in her every word, and her body movements also. The last thing he needed, though, was to have her walk out on him again. He knew that he'd always been a dog when it came to Tabora, or any other woman for that matter, but Janet was his rock. In reality Janet was the one who forgave him after each time he went out to play. But he knew that there was no way he could tell her that his fight at the office was all about a disk of him and Tabora, at least not now.

"Okay. Let's see, where do I begin?"

"Try beginning with what made a fight break out in a downtown law office." Janet so boldly interjected.

Omar stared at her with squinted eyes. What was wrong with the woman, he thought? She was really pushing her luck. He repositioned himself on the bed.

"Yeah whatever," he said, showing signs of irritability, he began at the top. "When Dunn repeated to me what he'd said to me earlier that day, I hit him before I knew it."

"Wait, goddamn you, I'm confused. What did he say to make you hit him?"

"Look, I don't want to see you hurting before I finish, so I'll tell you what was said after I finish telling you what happened, okay?"

"Sure." Janet shrugged her shoulders and turned to sat in the stuffed chair in the corner of the room. She pretended to be calm, but she was dying inside wanting to know what it was Dunn had said. It must have been something about her, and all she could picture was her man defending her honor.

"I looked at him on the floor like the punk that he is, and I started to kick his honky ass, but I didn't. Instead, I picked his ass up off the floor and said: 'if you say some shit like that about my wife again I'll kick your ass again.' I pushed him into the bar and all the glasses fell to the floor and broke."

"Hold up, babe. Did you say that he said something about me?"

"Yes, but I told you to wait until I was finished."

She called him babe. That was a far cry from talking about not staying the night with him. Omar knew then that all he had to do was push the right story to her and she would forget all the talk about rape and not coming back home to him. Now if he was able to get the disk from Dunn's office somehow, before he decided to show it to Janet or anyone else, that would put an end to his fears of him losing Janet.

"I turned to leave his office when he snuck behind me and punched me on my jaw from behind. When I fell, I heard the door open. The next thing I knew I was in the hallway, outside of his office with everyone looking on. The funny thing is no one saw me when I beat his ass inside of his office, but that's okay because before he sucker punched me I had beat his ass, but good," Omar finally said.

"What could Marc have said about me that was so bad? I've always thought that he was a jerk, but he seemed all right otherwise."

"You've got to promise me that you won't say anything to him, and you're going to let me continue to handle it, okay?"

"Okay boo. It won't be much of a big deal now that you've already kicked his butt, but good."

Janet smiled proudly at her man sitting on the bed across the room from her. She couldn't walk back out of that door now. Her man had just lost his job defending her honor, more than likely, and now he needed her. She sat back in the chair and listened as he explained what sent him through the roof and caused him to crush his boss's ass.

"He said that if I had let him sleep with my cute whore for a wife, perhaps I would have gotten the Tanner case. Babe, before I knew it I was off the chair and on his ass. I know I should have thought about it first."

"Oh, hh. No sweetheart, I'm so proud of you."

Janet rose to her feet and hurried across the room to where Omar sat on the side of the bed. She straddled her legs around his and leaned into him while he sat on the edge of the bed. His face was pressed against her breast. He kissed her in spite of the throbbing pain he felt when he puckered his swollen lips. He laid down as she crawled atop him. He removed his shirt then helped her to remove her blouse and bra. He attempted to roll her over.

"No daddy, let me take care of you tonight. Is that okay? I mean, can I do things to my man that I've never done to him before?"

"Sure sweetheart, but you don't have to. I know that you're angry with me."

"Shush."

Janet leaned over and turned the bedside lamp off and began to undress him in the dark, one item at a time.

10

In the plush residential community of Mount Vernon, Virginia, where luxurious homes sat back, away from the winding, hilly streets that lead to their beauty, and where many professional couples liked to call home, everyone seemed content with minding their own business. The areas were the perfect location for entertaining friends, private parties, and even the well attended outdoor lawn functions went unnoticed. Neighbors were situated distances away, one from the other, which created a sense of calm, quiet privacy, and that was exactly what attracted the Dunns' to the area. Being private people themselves, they could not have asked for anyplace better.

A golden evening sun had just given way to a grey, balmy night, and Tisha, Marc's wife, had decided to stay home to spend some badly needed time together with him. The Dunns lounged around near their newly renovated opened kitchen area when the door bell chimed softly throughout the house. Marc Dunn glanced over at his wife mysteriously before he removed his glasses from his face and rose to his feet; she shrugged her shoulders and simulated a smile then turned and lowered her head toward the book in her hands.

"I'll get it, hun," Marc said to his wife of four years. It was seven thirty P.M., and he nor his wife was expecting anyone over. Still, Larry,

Mr. J. from the office, sometimes stopped over to talk shop with his younger partner before heading home himself, but he hadn't popped in lately, and Marc felt that it was because of the friction between them, brought on by office politics; tonight though, he wouldn't mind seeing his friend, since Larry had been out of town for the past month.

Tisha remained seated just off to the right from the kitchen, while Marc buttoned his shirt on his way to the door.

"Who is it?" he asked, with his left hand on the door knob, and poised to open the door.

"It's me, Kelly."

The voice on the other side of the door sounded low, but it rang in Marc's ear like a train whistle.

"Kelly?" he muttered. He looked behind him, and hoped that Tisha had not walked up and heard the stranger's name, she would never understand, he thought; he never wanted her to know about his secret ties to the lowly drug world, and thugs like Big Kelly. "What in hell is *he* doing at my home?" he blurted openly, then swung the door open angrily.

"Who is it Marc?" Tisha's voice echoed from the kitchen area.

"Au, it's Larry dear, I'll only be a minute," he lied.

Big Kelly loomed large in the center of the doorway, and he had a nervous grin plastered on his face.

Tisha rose to her feet and headed toward the front door to properly invite Mr. J. in for a moment, because she knew Marc wouldn't think to do so; they would sometimes step outside and talk.

"What in hell is going on here, and what is so important that you have to show up at my home?" Marc shouted as loud as his whispering yell would allow. He looked at Big Kelly with serious discontent and thought that if the son of a bitch was fifty, or maybe sixty pounds lighter, he'd be planting his foot in Kelly's ass right now.

"You know it's ironic that you told your wife that I was Mr. J.," Big Kelly said, but before his poetic rendering was completed, an angry Marc interjected.

"Yeah, well state your business and be gone, and I'll deal with Larry's ass in the morning, he knows better than to resort to this type of shit." Marc barked.

Big Kelly all but ignored Marc, and with his chin lifted high, he peered through Marc's front door; he checked to insure no one else looked on from inside, Mrs. Dunn, he thought, would be at work in the hospital, so he now had to be brief, and possibly won't be able to search the house as planned. He calmly reached his right hand behind his back and pulled out his .45 semiautomatic.

Marc's eyes widened, and his life flashed before him. "What?" he mumbled. This couldn't be real, he thought. "What are you doing," he asked? And had no intention of awaiting an answer. He attempted to slam the door and run, but Big Kelly stood firm against the meager force of Marc's fear. He raised the pistol and fired it twice, hitting Marc in his back with both rounds.

Tisha, who had just stepped into their large foyer through the doorway on the right, screamed at the sight of her husband's body when it fell helplessly to the floor with a crude thump. She screamed again when she looked up at the huge black intruder; she instinctively turned to run for her life.

"Au shit," Big Kelly murmured. He looked anxiously behind him, toward the street, and it was all clear; he gave her a slow yet a resolute chase. He caught Mrs. Dunn at the foot of the stairs and pulled her backwards by her hair; she fell to the floor still screaming loudly. Big Kelly stood over her and looked around frantically until he leaned over and picked up a pillow from a nearby chair against the wall; the two shots were plenty enough noise, and he didn't want a third shot to attract any attention. He covered the weapon and stood directly over her as she pushed herself backward, away from him. He shadowed her every move.

"Please, no, please don't hurt me," she begged. Looking over both her shoulders as she slid backwards, but there was no where to run. She fell back and lay with her arms covering her face.

Though Mr. J. hadn't sent Big Kelly to the Dunns household to kill Mrs. Dunn, however, she had become a witness to the murder of her husband, and could identify Big Kelly. She had to die, and Big Kelly knew it from the time she placed her foot in the foyer. He fired twice at point blank range, striking her in her chest. Big Kelly stood to the side of Tisha and pushed her body with his foot in search of life, she didn't feel a thing, he reasoned.

He closed the front door and began a hour and a half search of the house that discovered nothing that would link Mr. J. to any drug dealings or murders. Big Kelly figured if Marc had any such evidence, then he must have passed in on already. Then he experienced an epiphany, "ah, hah, unless he already gave it to that broad Tabora?"

* * *

Tabora reported to work early the next morning after seeing reports of the double murder on the ten p.m. news last evening. She'd hardly slept a wink last night for fear of losing her own life. It was also reported that a witness driving pass Marc Dunn's home saw a large black man standing beside a parked car in front of their home earlier that evening; Tabora's mind ran rampant with visions of Big Kelly. She figured if Big Kelly was involved, then he certainly wasn't acting on his own accord, and she knew first hand about the rift between Mr. Jasper and Mr. Dunn, when he was alive. Was Mr. Jasper really was as Dangerous as Mr. Dunn had told her he was? She wasn't sure one way or the other, but in light of the murders, she too had formulated an agenda all her own.

Tabora stepped into the firm's main lobby and placed her purse beside the chair where she sat, and had but one thing on her mind: she wanted the infamous disk of her and Omar from Mr. Dunn's office before the police or someone else gained access to it.

The long carpeted hallway leading to Mr. Dunn's office reeked of eerie quietness as Tabora walked nervously to the office door. Her head swivelled left then right with a glance before entering the office. She stopped immediately and her head jerked to her left; she thought she heard movement out in the hall, toward Mr. Jasper's office, but continued into the office seconds later; no one else was ever there that early but her, she thought.

Behind his desk she had thoughts of how badly the womanizing prick treated her sometimes, and how sweet and caring he was at other times; she would miss him just the same. "Marc," she murmured. She smelled him in the still office air, as if he sat in the chair she leaned on.

She snapped out of her day dream to lean down and open the top right drawer of his desk. There was a pistol, a television's remote control, and a disk baring her name beneath the pistol. She raised the pistol gingerly and removed the disk, then quickly slid the disk down the front of her jeans, and closed the drawer.

Before walking away, however, Tabora leaned down and opened the drawer again. She retrieved a photograph that she thought she'd seen of her and Marc from the rear of the drawer; she smiled. As she pushed the drawer closed with her leg, but quickly, without thinking, she removed the pistol, and slid it down the small of her back; her blouse concealed both articles sufficiently upon her inspection. While looking at the photo, she turned toward the window. The wells of her eyes filled and caused tears to roll down her cheeks –

The office door suddenly opened. Tabora flinched and turned around drying her eyes.

"Oh, Tabora, I didn't know that you were in here, dear. I guess you heard?"

"Yes, Joyce, I heard."

"Well, I've got to go to the main lobby and pick up some boxes to pack his office. Would you do me a favor and lock the door when you leave out, dear," Joyce asked?

Tabora knew that she and Mr. Dunn's secret relationship wasn't all that secret, but she could tell that Joyce must have known, and that's why she allowed her the time inside of his office. She'd stayed long enough, though, and stepped out into the hallway.

She heard voices again, and they came from the end of the hallway, near Mr. Jasper's office; she didn't know that he'd come in already; what's more important, she had no idea just how dangerous he was until she over heard parts of his conversation; she walked softly toward the sound.

"So let's forget about the sloppy work you did last night," Mr. J. said, "as long as it does not come back to haunt us, of course."

"Okay, Mr. J., but like I said, I had no way of knowing that his wife would be home." Big Kelly replied.

Tabora thought that Big Kelly sounded nervous, and not as confident as he does when he comes into the office flirting with her.

"Listen, I don't know how much he may have told that broad of his, and I don't trust her. Hey, push that door." Mr. J. waited while Big Kelly closed the office door.

Tabora turned and walked stealthily and ever so briskly back to her station in the lobby. Nervously, she reached back and removed the gun, and placed it in the purse; all she could think of was the possibility that Mr. J. was speaking about her to Big Kelly, and she didn't have a chance to hear what he said. She removed the disk and pushed it into her purse also. Now she sat wondering why in hell did she take the gun? Though she lacked experience with guns, one thing was certain in her mind now: if she had to use the gun, she figured it wouldn't take much to put her finger between that hole and push that trigger. "And I would too," she muttered, in an attempt to convince herself.

"Hey, sweety," Big Kelly said.

Tabora literally jumped from her chair. "Huh, oh, hh, Mr. Kelly, you scared me," she said, nervously.

"I can see that, I'm sorry. I came in a little early, you know, to see Mr. J. Got this little case you know? Hey, how about the two of us going out some time, yo?"

If he thinks he's going to take her somewhere and bury her body alive, or whatever, he's sadly mistaking, she reasoned, then lied. "Well, I can't, but thanks anyway," she said, then flipped conversation to verbiage. "Did you hear about Mr. Dunn? It's sad isn't it. He and his poor wife were both taken at the same time" –

"Yeah, well, look, think about us, and I'll give you a call soon."

* * *

Omar who was at his home in Virginia that morning, snuck downstairs to the den while Janet prepared for work, he went straight to the telephone and dialed the law firm.

* * *

"Okay, but I'm very busy for most of the next few weeks," Tabora said to Big Kelly, and she watched as he walked out to the elevators; she remembered when there was a time she would have given Big Kelly. The phone rang.

Tabora flinched in her seat, she had to take a moment to settle her jumpy nerves. "Shit, what is wrong with me this morning," she mumbled to herself. She cleared her throat.

"Good morning, Dunn, Hope, Jasper & Browns, how may I direct your call, please?" Tabora asked.

"Good morning," Omar said, low toned and suavely; he needed Tabora's help and didn't want anything to go wrong.

"Omar?"

"Yes, babe, it's me. Hey I'm sorry to hear about Marc and his wife, but I can't lie to you, I don't feel shit for the white boy."

"Well, that figures, and is to be expected, I guess." Tabora responded. "Are you calling for Mr. Jasper again? It seems the two of you talk more now than when you worked here."

"Hey, he's trying to help me out, but no, this call is for you, sweetheart." He cleared his throat. "Hey, au, do you think you can get into Marc's office and get that disk, you know, before someone else gets their hands on it," he asked.

Tabora felt in her heart that she owed it to Omar to tell him she had the disk, yet she thought about it momentarily, then answered.

"I've already got the disk, Omar, and I intend to destroy it," she admitted.

"No, I mean, I have to see it being destroyed, do you understand me?"

"I don't know about that, Omar, and I'm not even sure if I trust you anymore."

In the meantime, Janet walked into the bedroom after her morning shower, and stood naked in front of the mirror. Still reeling from the new found sexual experiences she's allowed herself to partake in with Omar ever since he told her of the heroic stance he took at work in her honor. She thought of how all she wanted to do now was fulfill his every fantasy from now on. But then she saw the reflection of a red light flashing on the telephone next to the bed behind her. "Who is he talking to," she wondered? After retrieving the towel and wrapping her body, she walked cautiously to the bed and sat next to the phone.

With skills of a cat burglar, she eased the receiver up from it's base and carefully placed her hand over the microphone. She listened intently.

"I know no one's going to work all day today due to the Dunn's deaths, so why don't you come over here at, au, hh, one thirty today. Janet will be at work, and won't be a problem."

"Oh, really."

"Yeah, babe, but I've got to hang up now. I'll be waiting for you, woman."

Janet quickly lowered the receiver and rushed back into the bathroom, where Omar would believe she'd been all along. "That son of a bitch is gonna bring one of his sluts into my house while I'm out working, huh? Well we'll see about that shit." She said, angrily.

"Wait, don't hang up," Tabora shouted. "I don't want to come to your house, because that would be disrespectful to your wife. Don't you think so?"

"No, babe, this is business," he replied, "and I need to be certain that the disk is destroyed, okay? And listen to you, all respectful and shit. Baby look, even if the bitch was here, this is Omar's house, and I'll invite over whomever I please," he concluded, brimming with confidence.

"I'll think about it, Omar," Tabora said. "I've got to go, Joyce is coming and I want to speak with her. I'll call you."

"Hey wait, why don't you go ahead and put me through to Mr. Jasper, would you do that for me, please?"

"Sure, no problem."

Joyce hadn't returned from the downstairs lobby yet, as Tabora had so graciously lied. Instead, she needed time to think, to gather her thoughts. Big Kelly loomed heavily on her mind; was she next on his hit list? Lord. She hoped not. If she was right in assuming that Mr. J. and Big Kelly were the culprits behind the Dunns' murders, then the clandestine drug ring at the law firm had to be much bigger than she'd ever imagined. While seated at her desk, she began to wonder how much did they think she knew about their business, and what was so important about it that they would kill for it to keep? –

"Tabora, Tabora, are you all right?"

"Hum, oh, hh, Joyce, what did you say?" Tabora asked.

"I said that Mr. Jasper is going to close the office in another hour, and said that you can leave now, though. All business is cancelled except today's court cases. Girl, you look like you could use the time off. Go ahead, get out of here." Joyce ordered.

"I do need the time off, but I'll be all right."

* * *

Taylor sat all alone in the secured room inside of the Richmond, Virginia, mental institution where she was placed for observation. The State could only assume to know what must have taken place at her home on the night of her father's brutal murder. Blood had splattered throughout the bedroom, and Taylor was found incoherent, covered in blood and still holding the knife in her trembling hand. Though it was early in the case, her doctors and legal representation were not sure if she would ever be well enough to testify in her own defense.

However, anyone with just a little knowledge of such cases knew that the Commonwealth of Virginia, in their eagerness to avenge a murder, would medicate lowly prisoners in an attempt to try them as sane and capable of standing trial in a court of law. Sara hoped that

Taylor's case was not considered big enough a case for them to subject Taylor to such treatment, because if they did, and Taylor started talking, she would be in a lot of trouble for not sticking around to turn herself into the police that night. All she could think about now was getting back to Maryland, around friends and family, until the episode with Taylor blows over.

11

After calling Omar, Tabora drove into Virginia straight from work in the District. She was frightened, and yet there was this feeling of obligation that she felt toward Omar; she felt that it was her fault the tape was ever recorded, not to mention the lost of his job. After the tape is destroyed, however, Omar would be on his own, and her self-imposed obligation to him will be fulfilled, she reasoned, as she neared his home.

At the same time Tabora felt sad over the lost of the Dunn family, especially Marc, she didn't know his wife at all, though she felt she did; Marc spoke of her often enough when they were together. The more she thought about it, the more she felt that it must be her calling to commit herself to a period of soul searching. It was just a short time ago that she lost Chad, and now Marc. She'd already decided that her late night episodes with strangers for sex, had gotten too dangerous to continue. She had been rape twice, and gang banged by up to four men at least three times. She was at the end of her rope when it came to men, and felt that it was time that she resorted to her old childhood remedy; masturbation was safe and she was in control. Speaking of control, she thought of Omar, if she never saw him again after today, it would be no great loss to her. She smiled as she pulled onto the right side of his double driveway. "Omar needs to keep his nasty behind home with his wife," she murmured.

Omar, she thought, was older and also funny, and oh did he know how to deliver in bed, but he lied so much and also had a terrible mean streak. "No," she muttered, "I couldn't trust him anymore, not even for the sex," she concluded.

* * *

"I told you that there would be a place for you here at the firm, and I ve kept my word to you , Omar," Mr. J. said. "Now I'm afraid that it's your turn to keep your end of the bargain."

"I know, Mr. J., I'm just not sure that I can go through with it," Omar admitted.

"Stop right there, Omar. Now you came to me for help in getting your job back, and I told you how we were going to make that happen. Now what you need to do is stop whining like a little bitch, and pull yourself together.

"With Marc out of the way, you'll become partner right away. This is a young law firm but our future is riding on your sticking to the plan. I've let her off early and Kelly is following her to your house as we speak. So do your job and he'll come in and remove the body." Mr. J. slammed the receiver down. "Sorry sack of shit," he muttered.

"Damn," Omar said openly, and places both his hands up to his head. "What the hell have I gotten myself into?" He waited for Tabora to arrive.

Janet was determined to be there in time to catch lying ass Omar in the act of making love to another woman in their home, and as angrily as she is now while headed home, she wasn't sure what the outcome would be. It seemed the more she wiped tears from her swollen eyes, the more her tears flooded her vision. She drove and balled her eyes out. She had thought to stay around the neighborhood until Tabora arrived, but later decided to go to work and take of the half day.

"All that I've been through with him," she said openly, "I'll kill his ass before I except that from him."

Janet cried like a baby, and looked down at the pistol, belonging to Omar, that lay on the seat next to her, and she thought that if she couldn't have him all to herself, then no one will have him. She cried harder.

All of this sneaking around comes on the heels of her finally succumbing to being his love slave, all she could think about now is how he made her do things in bed that she never imagined doing before. What was sad about it, though, she couldn't bring herself to say that she didn't enjoy every second of him masterfully having his way with her. She sighed and shivered in her seat. "Oh, Lord," she cried.

Big Kelly had followed Tabora, undetected, over to Omar's house. He had no idea where she would lead him to, but he hoped that it was to Omar's house so that the plan could finally take place, and he could then retrieve the body and place it where it will never be found, just as Mr. J. instructed him to do; Mr. J. felt that if Tabora's body was never found, then the firm would have less attention placed on it. For the moment Big Kelly sat in the black sports utility vehicle across from the Johnson's front yard.

* * *

"Come on in, girl, damn you're looking good," Omar said, as he opened the door for Tabora to come into his home.

He smiled and tried to show calmness as she entered, but he had a lot on his mind. He'd gone to the bedroom to get his pistol to position it in the den, where he planned to take Tabora, but the pistol was missing; he couldn't pop-a-cap on her now, and had to come up with some other way of killing her, but quick.

That same old weasel's smile, and ancient charm, this old fella will never change, Tabora thought, as she walked in and saw Omar for the first time since his beat down at the office. "Thank you, Omar, but like I said, I'm only here to deliver the disk and watch it get destroyed."

"No problem, babe, and I appreciate your coming. So, may I have the disk?" Tabora reached into her purse to retrieve the disk when she felt the gun that she'd forgot she took from Mr. Dunn's desk drawer. She looked up at Omar with her hand on the pistol, and it made her feel good to know that she had some means of protection; not that she would need it with Omar, she thought. She handed him the disk.

"Okay then, follow me to the den babe. I want to show you something."

"No, Omar, look I don't think I should" –

"Hey, hey, you have my word as a gentleman, I only want to show you something, and it's right there in the den," he said.

In the den Omar place the disk in the machine and turned it on. He smiled and turned to Tabora.

"I got to be sure that this is the right disk, you know. Sit yourself and your purse down in the chair, woman, shit, you're making me nervous," he said, and smiled.

Tabora was reluctant, but she placed her purse in the seat beside her. She thought about how once she would've wanted Omar all over her, all in her. Instead, she was proud of herself for being strong enough to finally let Omar go. He was old news. Then the picture of her and Omar came on the screen. She heard herself moaning, and saw his and her sweaty bodies with Omar firmly inside of her. He kissed her everywhere and it was as if she felt every kiss of his soft lips on her body; she got fidgety in her seat, and hoped that he did not notice her.

"Well, there's no doubt in my mind that it is the right disk," she said.

Omar laughed and walked over to where she sat, and he pulled her by the arm up from the chair and across the room to the sofa, where he threw her down.

"Stop, Omar," she screamed. She realized what was about to happen and couldn't believe it. She screamed louder. "Damn you, Omar, stop!"

"Don't worry babe. It'll be just like the old days. You see, if it wasn't for you, I wouldn't have to hurt you so bad."

"What? Get your ass off of me," she yelled. This was not one of those times that she would just lay still and close her eyes, because she was dead set on putting those days behind her, and Omar had damn well better known it, she thought.

Tabora punched Omar hard in his face with her right hand and kicked him backwards with her feet; he flipped backwards over the sofa's armrest, and onto the floor. She jumped up to make a run for it, but just as she passed by him, he sprang up and punched her with a solid left to her stomach.

"Come back here, bitch," he shouted.

"Ugh, hh," she fell to the floor crouched over, with both her arms at her stomach.

"Now you've made it where I don't mind killing your ass, girl," he said, while standing over her, undressing himself down to his bare ass. He then continued his assault.

Big Kelly watched from across the street as Janet placed her key in the front door of the house, and he could see that she was trying to be quiet as she tipped inside. He knew then that nothing good was going to come out of what he thought might be going on inside. He waited anyway, before phoning Mr. J.

Janet walked lightly, and could hear Tabora's screams. She took a position near the kitchen, and she could see the television set. She stood as if in shock, momentarily, before more tears built up in her eyes again; she'd seen the date near the bottom of the screen, and knew that there was no way Omar could lie his way out of this one. It was practically a new disk, and he was deeply involved in the moment.

When she finally snapped out of it, she realized he wasn't only deeply involved on the disk, but his naked ass was all over Tabora on the floor of the den, trying to force himself on her.

Omar was having a hard time with Tabora, who bravely fought him off of her, but he was relentless in his pursuit.

"Stop, you no-good son of a bitch. Stop!" Janet shouted. She was crying herself blind with tears, but held the pistol aimed directly at Omar, who'd jumped to his feet in shock.

Tabora rose to her feet straightening her clothing. "The bastard tried to rape me," she cried.

"Child, you need to get your shit and get the hell out of here, now," Janet said. She'd stopped crying long enough to order Tabora out of her house, but she never took her water soaked eyes off of Omar.

"You're a sorry, pathetic ass fool, and you wouldn't know a good woman, you bastard, if one knocked you down," Janet said, with the pistol pointed at his chest.

"Baby, look," Omar said, "it wasn't what you think, I was just playing around, and she'll tell you. Wasn't I Tabora?" Omar seemed desperate in his attempts to get Tabora to support his lie, but she was far from in the mood, and so was Janet.

"Stop, Omar," is all Janet could bring herself to say to him.

"Yeah, and that's the disk that caused him to get beat up at the office, and lose his job," Tabora said. He had never pissed her off as badly as he had when he tried to rape her, and she heard him when he said that he would also kill her. She was telling it all. But she knew she had to get out of the house before Janet's angry rage turned on her.

Tabora rushed pass Janet and grabbed her purse on her way to the front door.

"Sweetheart, is that my gun?" Omar asked. He stood with his hands above his head as if he was under arrest, and tried to steer Janet to another conversation before she realized what Tabora had just told her; he'd never seen Janet as upset before, and she'd never held a gun on him before either.

Janet never answered Omar, in stead she walked over and removed the disk, and shattered it against the wall of the den.

"So you were fighting Marc over something he said about me, right Omar? And you beat his ass, didn't you baby?"

"Yeah babe, I told you, I did it all for you. Come on now, put the gun down."

"You stood by and watched me make a fool of myself with you over a lie that you told me," Janet said. She cried harder than before, until suddenly her eyes widened, and she let out a sigh while staring him in the eyes. "Lord, help me," she muttered.

While trying to get out of the front door, Tabora heard two shots . . . pop . . . pop. She screamed and her body flinched. Filled with fear, she hurried out to her car.

Janet stood over Omar, who seemed to hang onto some semblance of life, and her tears were all gone. Her face showed no expression as she looked down at him.

He reached his right hand out to her. "Babe, I love you," he said.

She simply reached out her left hand and grasped his out stretched hand. "I love you too, Boo," she whispered. Then she raised the pistol to her mouth with her trembling right hand, and while kneeling in front of him, she pulled the trigger. Her body fell next to his.

When Tabora heard the third shot, she burned rubber backing out of the driveway, and almost hit Big Kelly's truck in the process, he too was trying to get as far away from the house as he could. But she never saw his face through the smoked window tint.

Big Kelly wasn't waiting around to be implicated in another murder, especially since he wasn't responsible for any. But had Mr. J. not told him to dispense of Tabora's body, he thinks he would have taken her down just then, in the driveway. In stead, Tabora, unknowingly, followed Big Kelly until they reached interstate 95 north, anyway. While Big Kelly cruised over the Woodrow Wilson bridge into Maryland, Tabora slammed her accelerator and didn't slow down until she reached the Allentown Road exit. She was as nervous as could be, to think that just that fast Omar was probably dead, along with Janet. "What the hell is going on with all this killing?" she murmured.

Big Kelly watched and let her go, and figured he'd catch up to her later. He'd phoned Mr. J., and told him what he thought happened inside the house. Mr. J. instructed Big Kelly to back off of Tabora until they were sure of what took place inside.

12

Sara temporarily resided in Bowie, a Maryland suburb just minutes from downtown Washington, D.C., with her cousin Kenya, who had move to the area from New Orleans, Louisiana after hurricane Katrina. Sara hadn't told anyone, to include her parents, of her troubles in Virginia, involving Taylor and her father, or the fact that she'd dropped out of college with only one half year left to graduation and was still hold up in town.

Frankly, she thought for sure that she'd see Tabora at Omar's funeral services a week ago; she lied when she told her parents that it was Tabora who'd told her about Omar's death, and that is why she was already in town. She was surprise when only a couple of people from the law firm showed up, and Tabora wasn't one of them.

She sat in her bed room and thought for sure that after hearing how that crazy whore Janet had 'bugged-out', for no apparent reason, and killed poor Omar before turning the gun on herself, that everyone who knew him would show up to see him off; she couldn't understand why of all people, Tabora didn't show up to the funeral.

Now with nothing but idle time on her hands, Sara finds herself sitting around the house all the time, mopping over the recent tragedies in her life. She flinched when the door to her bedroom swung open, then Kenya walked in with a beer in her hand; she knew that something had to be troubling Kenya for her to barge in on her like that. She stared and anxiously waited.

"Oh, shit girl," Kenya said, her head repelled from the oder, and her face frowned. "When are you going to start taking your fucking ass up out of this room and doing something with yourself?" Kenya finally asked, in her usually crude manner. She fanned her nostrils as she walked further into the room. "And you need to clean this damn room, shit, it stinks in here, girl."

"Oh, hh, Kenya, you really need to work on getting some Sunday in that nasty mouth of yours," Sara replied.

"I don't give a shit about that, ho, and I thought you said you were gonna call that so-called friend of yours, what's her name?"

"Tabora, Kenya. Her name is Tabora, and I will call her this evening, after she gets off from work," Sara explained. "And so you'll know, she doesn't have a cell phone, so I have to wait until she gets home, okay?"

"Au huh, whatever, and didn't your ass tell me that you'd be staying here for a little while, damn-near a month ago? Look at you. You're growing roots under your lazy ass in this room. Get out of here, do something with yourself, like going back and finishing school," Kenya suggested.

Sara watched as Kenya hurriedly left the room and knew that she was right, she had to put her life back in order, and soon.. She'll call Tabora to see about paying her a visit later this evening, she decided. And after that, she figures to begin putting her life back on track.

* * *

Strangely enough, Tabora was still the receptionist at the law firm, and was surprised herself at how comfortable she'd been made to feel around the office as of late; considering how she once felt that her life was in danger, and she wouldn't survive through the night. Nothing could be further from the truth, her time spent around the office is fine, it couldn't be better. Consequently, she now often wondered what it was that made her feel that, Mr. J. and Big Kelly were out to get her, or anyone else for that matter. She reasoned that the two of them were not talking about hurting anyone that morning, and she hadn't heard what it was she thought she'd heard.

"Ms Yarborough," Tabora shouted to the crowd of clients seated in the lobby's waiting area. "Ms April Yarborough?"

"Yes, right here," a young lady raised her hand and shouted from the crowd.

"Okay, dear, Mr. Hunter will see you now. Its straight down the hall and to the right," Tabora said.

It was Friday and all had been going well at the office when Tabora put her head down to check Ms Yarborough's name from her waiting list. She heard the lobby's door open and shut, but paid it no mind until she'd completed adjusting her waiting list of clients. She raised her head with her usual smile, until her eyes swept upward and met those of the client, who leaned down over the counter.

"Mr. Kelly, you frightened me," Tabora said, holding her chest with her right hand. "How can I help you today?"

"I came to see Mr. Jasper, and he told me to come straight in, but I wanted to say hello to you, sweetheart," Big Kelly said, in almost a whisper, where only Tabora could hear him. And she was fine with that, until she noticed the eerie grin displayed on his face, along with the fact that his right hand hung below the counter, out of view of the other clients, with his index finger and thumb shaped a pistol. "Pow, I'll see you later, girl," he whispered, and stared back at her with grave intend.

She made an attempt at smiling, and could feel the twitching in her facial muscles. Why is he doing this, she thought? She looked around in hopes that no one noticed, but the feeling of nervousness and concern had already caused the tiny hairs on her arms to stand up. Her body shivered for just that instant.

It was five thirty, and already dark out. The night air was cool, and a southerly wind blew softly against the trees just outside of Tabora's apartment window in the back. The hard dry leaves strewn about the small patio out back caused haunting sounds each time the wind kicked up just a little, and a frightened Tabora, who was all alone inside, flinched nervously each time the dry leaves were stirred up. She tried to tell herself that there was nothing to be afraid of, but as soon as she did, and made herself believe it, the phone rang.

Oh, good, she thought, here was her chance to talk to someone, and perhaps calm her nerves in the process.

"Hello, hello," she removed the receiver from her ear and inspected it, then hit it against her left palm. "Hello, who is this," she asked?

When no one answered, she slammed the phone down. The dry leaves on the patio seemed to be trapped in a small wind funnel as they churned out of control against the patio door.

It was probably someone who dialed the wrong number. She told herself. But the phone rang again. She jumped, and released a short bursting scream. "Hello, hello." This time she slammed the phone down and ran straight for the bedroom, and with all the speed she could muster, she packed a bag.

Big Kelly had used that trick on many occasions in the past, but never had it worked so well as it did tonight. He didn't know it yet, but Tabora was upstairs in her apartment doing just what he needed her to do. Eliminating her and disposing of her body, should prove to be an easy assignment after all.

Tabora decided that this was it. She was going over to her mother's house in Camp Springs, and as much as she liked her independence, she was prepared to stay the entire weekend with her.

She piled enough things in a suit case to last her, then opened the door to the night stand beside her bed, when there was nothing there that she thought she'd need, she slammed it closed. "What was that," she murmured, and quickly reopened the door? She grabbed the manilla envelope. "A book from Marc?" she said openly. She searched her nervous mind, in vain, for the time she received the package from Marc. She threw it in her suit case and hurriedly completed packing her things. Once she finished, she looked around the apartment one last time before leaving. The phone rang once again. She stood and look at it, momentarily, then opted to let it rang this time.

"Come on, girl, answer the phone," Sara pleaded through the phone. She'd decided as a means of getting out of the house for a change, to just drive over and surprise Tabora with a visit. "Shit, Tabora, pick up."

She had come this far and decided that she may as well go to the apartment and maybe give Tabora a few minutes to get back from wherever she may have gone.

Tabora rushed out of the apartment and across the dimly lit parking lot. It was as spooky outside as it was in the apartment, and the wind caused eerie sounds all around Tabora. She inspected the trees along the sidewalk in front of her car, and hesitated when she thought she saw something. "Damn wind," she muttered. Her head swivelled quickly in both directions, while her eyes swept the area in the direction of every frightening sound. When she opened the rear door of her car, her body leaned forward, and with both her hands she slung the suit case inside to land where it may. She slammed the rear door and quickly opened the front door. Once inside, she placed her key in the ignition with her purse still hanging from her shoulder. Before starting the car she had an idea, and already she felt better.

She reached into her purse and removed the pistol that she'd started carrying as a kind of keepsake more than anything else, and she held it in her hand. "Yeah, come to mama, baby," she said, then turned to pull the door closed –

"Hey girl," Big Kelly shouted, as he leaned inside of her opened door.

Tabora turned to see his huge face inches from hers, and couldn't contain herself. She was so frightened, she screamed and all but lobbed the pistol from her hand into Big Kelly's chest. She watched the gun as it hit his arm and feel just outside of her car door. She screamed again.

Big Kelly leaned his huge body upward and punched her in her face with his left, tightly closed fist, and though lucid, Tabora was frightened into submission, momentarily.

"Get your ass out of the car," he ordered while pulling her upon her feet. "What do you know about a gun?"

During the madness, the gun was kicked next to the left front tire, just pass the door.

"What do you want, and where are you taking me?"

"Shut up, you ole fine thang you. Would you like it if I took you to my truck first," Big Kelly asked, brimming with sarcasm? He had Tabora firmly by her right arm, with his gun pointed toward her under the cover of darkness, and he pulled her along the tree-lined sidewalk that led to the far end of the parking lot, and Big Kelly's truck, which was shadowed by a lone dumpster.

"Don't worry babe, this won't hurt, and when I finish with your ass no one will find you."

Tabora saw what looked like the head lights of a car as it entered the parking lot. She screamed to the top of her voice.

"Shut up, I said. Look, I don't want to carry your blooded ass all the way across this lot, but I will if I have to. You better not say another word."

Big Kelly looked back and saw that the car had parked near where he'd just left. He didn't seem worried since his truck was parked in the direction that he was headed to; the area where he anticipated taking Tabora to meet her demise.

Sara never heard the screams that came from Tabora; due to the wind, her car windows were up, but when she parked and saw Tabora's car door opened, she ran over to investigate. Tabora's keys were still in the ignition and her purse had fallen from her shoulder onto the passenger's seat. Sara stood and squinted her eyes, with her chin raised, she could see that the person being pulled down the sidewalk was Tabora. She eased the car door closed and took a step toward the side walk in front of the car.

"What?" she said openly when she kicked something hard into the curb in front of her. She looked down and saw that it was a gun, and after further inspection, she realized that the gun was real, and loaded.

Sara didn't appear to have a plan when she ran, with the gun in her hand from tree to tree, in an all-out effort to catch up to Tabora and the big stranger attached to her.

As they neared the dumpster, Tabora had a good idea of what her life expectancy was, and she'd made up her mind to die trying to escape rather than walking peacefully into death. When they reached the end of the paved area, she used her right shoulder to push Big Kelly with everything she had, into a car parked on the end. Big Kelly, apparently caught of guard, stumbled down the curb into the parking lot, and seemed to sprain his ankle in the process; he yelled and grabbed his right ankle.

"Ugh, shit, oh, hh," Big Kelly let out a loud growl that seemed to echo throughout the apartment buildings.

Tabora slipped among the dry leaves before regaining her balance, and ran back towards her vehicle.

Big Kelly bolted up to his feet, and favoring his right foot, he took aim at Tabora and fired one round.

Tabora screamed and fell hard to the ground. Holding her left shoulder, she made an attempt to rise to her feet and run.

Big Kelly took aim again. "The game is over, honey," he yelled.

But before he fired, his eyes widened when he heard the sound, then saw the flash of fire that came from the silhouette standing along the side of the tree across from him . . . Pop

"Shit," was all he could muster before the hot lead entered his chest. He flinched, then froze, momentarily. He bravely turned and took aim on the stranger by the tree. But he seemed to smile when he saw not one, but two flashes, one after the other, his face reflected the pain as it rippled through his chest and stomach.

Tabora heard the sounds and screamed, and had no idea what had just happened.

Big Kelly dropped his aim. Dead on his feet, he fell to his knees, then buckled over between the two cars where he stood.

"Tabora," Sara shouted. "Come this way, girl, and let's get out of here."

"Sara?" Tabora muttered, then she added, "Sara, I'm shot, and what are you doing here?" Tabora cried, then looked over towards Big Kelly. "Is he dead?"

"Damn, Tabora, one thing at a time, and you're not dead, now come on, let's go."

She ran over and grabbed Tabora and helped her to her feet. "Get your ass up, girl, and let me see your arm. Shit, you're not even bleeding," Sara said.

"But it burns," Tabora replied before they both took off running.

The two women ran along the back of the apartment building until they worked their way back to the other side, and blended in with a few onlookers before going back up to Tabora's apartment. Tabora grabbed a few more items of hers, and felt strongly that she would not be back to the apartment for a while after what took place tonight.

13

In Bowie later that night the two friends had cleaned themselves up, and Sara had just walked her cousin Kenya to the front door to see her off to work.

"I don't want the two of you 'Hos tearing my house up, now, and I'll see you in the morning. And keep my damn door locked." Kenya shouted, pulling out of the driveway.

"Yeah, yeah, okay, now go," Sara replied.

"Wow, look at you," Sara said when she walked in and saw Tabora lying in bed with only a robe on. Her left knee was elevated, and the robe was opened and pulled down below the wound on her shoulder; her naked body was exposed.

"Girl, I'm trying to see the bullet hole in my arm,"

Sara walked over and sat next to her on the bed and removed Tabora's arm from the robe. "Please, Tabora, this is not even a flesh wound. It's more like a skin burn, if anything," Sara said. She stared at Tabora's caramel flesh then turned and kissed the palm of Tabora's hand that she held. "Let me make it all better for you," Sara offered. She left a line of kisses from Tabora's palm to the skin burn on her arm.

Confused, Tabora smiled awkwardly at first, then closed her eyes when Sara's right hand cupped her breast. "Uh, hh, wee, shit, you're making it feel good all over," Tabora admitted.

Sara, in an attempt to reposition herself, caused Tabora's suit case to fall to the floor and sprang open. "Oops," Sara said. "I better pick that up before I forget and end up hearing Kenya's mouth in the morning."

The first item she saw was the manilla envelope. "Marc Dunn? What is this, a book of some sort?" she asked.

"I don't know, but just put it right there, and I'll look at it in a minute or so," Tabora said. "Right now I would love it if you'd continue making me feel better."

Sara's bright eyes widened and she smiled. She place the articles back into the opened suit case with out paying much attention to what she was doing, and climbed back into bed.

"I've always loved you," she said to Tabora.

Tabora smiled awkwardly and replied, "And I've always loved you too."

"No, you don't understand," Sara said. She leaned down and kissed Tabora's breast, and began working her way to Tabora's neck.

"Um, mm, oh, wait," Tabora said with slurred words. She leaned over and turned off the lamp beside the bed, and laid back down. And there she was, likened to the darkness of her own bed room. Sara wasted no time resuming where she'd left off, and soon Tabora reciprocated. She had gone full circle in her secret quest to fulfill the never ending desires of her monstrous sexual appetite.

Printed in the United States
200476BV00001B/1-105/A

9 781434 349170